"Storm's here," Logan said.

It had been a long time since Annie had had *any* storms in her life—this one just happened to be a physical storm, rather than an emotional one. And she'd survived the emotional ones.

More or less.

She tilted her head to look up at Logan, only to find the dark cast of his eyes watching her through the gloomy light.

Annie was suddenly aware of the intimacy of their positions. Of the fact that his chest was pressed against her back. Hard, wide and feeling damnably perfect.

The kind of chest that could shelter her.

And had. Impossible memories of his warm touch, his rough sighs, slipped into her mind. Impossible, because he'd turned her away all those years ago. Impossible, because what they'd shared had lived only in her dreams.

His long fingers skimmed over her cheek and her mouth went dry. She shuddered and the warmth of him became something else entirely.

Dear Reader,

Breeze into fall with six rejuvenating romances from Silhouette Special Edition! We are happy to feature our READERS' RING selection, *Hard Choices* (SE#1561), by favorite author Allison Leigh, who writes, "I wondered about the masks people wear, such as the 'good' girl/boy vs. the 'bad' girl/boy, and what ultimately hardens or loosens those masks. Annie and Logan have worn masks that don't fit, and their past actions wouldn't be considered ideal behavior. I hope readers agree this is a thought-provoking scenario!"

We can't get enough of Pamela Toth's WINCHESTER BRIDES miniseries as she delivers the next book, *A Winchester Homecoming* (SE#1562). Here, a world-weary heroine comes home only to find her former flame ready to reignite their passion. MONTANA MAVERICKS: THE KINGSLEYS returns with Judy Duarte's latest, *Big Sky Baby* (SE#1563). In this tale, a Kingsley cousin comes home to find that his best friend is pregnant. All of a sudden, he can't stop thinking of starting a family…with her!

Victoria Pade brings us an engagement of convenience and a passion of *in*convenience, in *His Pretend Fiancée* (SE#1564), the next book in the MANHATTAN MULTIPLES miniseries. Don't miss *The Bride Wore Blue Jeans* (SE#1565), the last in veteran Marie Ferrarella's miniseries, THE ALASKANS. In this heartwarming love story, a confirmed bachelor flies to Alaska and immediately falls for the woman least likely to marry! In *Four Days, Five Nights* (SE#1566) by Christine Flynn, two strangers are forced to face a growing attraction when their small plane crashes in the wilds.

These moving romances will foster discussion, escape and lots of daydreaming. Watch for more heart-thumping stories that show the joys and complexities of a woman's world.

Happy reading!

Karen Taylor Richman,
Senior Editor

Please address questions and book requests to:
Silhouette Reader Service
U.S.: 3010 Walden Ave., P.O. Box 1325, Buffalo, NY 14269
Canadian: P.O. Box 609, Fort Erie, Ont. L2A 5X3

Hard Choices

ALLISON LEIGH

SPECIAL **EDITIO**N™

Published by Silhouette Books

America's Publisher of Contemporary Romance

For my daughters, Amanda and Anna Claire.
Always a joy, continually challenging
and the greatest of blessings.

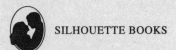 SILHOUETTE BOOKS

ISBN 0-373-24561-0

HARD CHOICES

Copyright © 2003 by Allison Lee Davidson

Visit Silhouette at www.eHarlequin.com

Printed in U.S.A.

Books by Allison Leigh

Silhouette Special Edition

Stay... #1170
The Rancher and the Redhead #1212
A Wedding for Maggie #1241
A Child for Christmas #1290
Millionaire's Instant Baby #1312
Married to a Stranger #1336
Mother in a Moment #1367
Her Unforgettable Fiancé #1381
The Princess and the Duke #1465
Montana Lawman #1497
Hard Choices #1561

*Men of the Double-C Ranch

ALLISON LEIGH

started early by writing a Halloween play that her grade-school class performed. Since then, though her tastes have changed, her love for reading has not. And her writing appetite simply grows more voracious by the day.

She has been a finalist in the RITA® Award and the Holt Medallion contests. But the true highlights of her day as a writer are when she receives word from a reader that they laughed, cried or lost a night of sleep while reading one of her books.

Born in Southern California, Allison has lived in several different cities in four different states. She has been, at one time or another, a cosmetologist, a computer programmer and a secretary. She has recently begun writing full-time after spending nearly a decade as an administrative assistant for a busy neighborhood church, and currently makes her home in Arizona with her family. She loves to hear from her readers, who can write to her at P.O. Box 40772, Mesa, AZ 85274-0772.

Dear Reader,

I love books. I love to read them, puzzle over them, agree with them and disagree with them. But not until the past several years did I realize that in my process of devouring and enjoying these books, I was missing one particularly enjoyable element of the reading experience: discussing. And, interestingly enough, we readers, we lovers of books, don't have to necessarily agree with each other about what a particular book is saying. That's the beauty of it. We each take away from what we've read something distinctly individual. But even in the differences, we tend to find our common ground with one another. In the process of discussing a book, we take an activity that is ordinarily rather solitary and we touch others. And that, in a nutshell, is one of the reasons why I love to write. To reach out and, in some small way, touch someone.

Needless to say, I was particularly honored and pleased to learn that *Hard Choices* would be part of the Readers' Ring. I hope you enjoy reading Logan and Annie's story. I also hope the questions at the back of this book will jump-start your own enjoyable discussions!

Best wishes, and happy reading.

Allison

Prologue

"Don't."

She nearly sagged with relief at the deep voice that came out of the darkness. But she didn't sag too long; she took advantage of Drago's momentary surprise and twisted out of his loosened grip. The whitewashed stucco snagged at her dress as she pushed away from where he'd pinned her into the corner outside the boathouse.

Drago's surprise didn't last long, though. His hand shot out and sank into her hair, yanking her back toward him. She cried out, twisting her ankle as she tipped back, scrabbling at his hold on her. Tears stung her eyes. Her skin crawled as his mouth touched her cheek.

"I said, *don't.*" The voice came again.

It was all she could do not to whimper—in pain at

the agonizing pull of Drago's hand on her hair, in relief that maybe her own stupidity wasn't going to be the end of her, after all.

The moment seemed excruciatingly clear. Drago's breath on her cheek. Her own whistling between her clenched teeth. And the faint scrape of a shoe on the damp walkway.

Her rescuer.

She shifted, trying to alleviate the pressure on her scalp. "Let go of me, Drago. I warned you to leave me alone."

He laughed softly, and slid one hand over her hip. "We had a deal, baby doll. Remember?"

She wriggled against his grip. "And the deal's off. You're dealing dr—ah!" She fell back against him at another vicious pull on her hair. She opened her mouth to scream, but suddenly, she was free. She stumbled, tried to right herself, but failed. She threw her hands backward to catch herself, but the sidewalk still met her rear with teeth-jarring force, and fresh tears clogged her throat, stung her nose.

Her hair streamed across her face. The curls she'd painstakingly ironed smooth were springing back to life in the damp air and she watched through them as Drago scrambled up from where he, too, had hit the sidewalk.

The man who stood over Drago was tall. Taller, even, than her brother, Will, who topped six feet. And he was dark. She didn't need the golden light cast by the iron lampposts to tell her that his dark hair was just shy of ebony, or that he was tanned. Not a cultivated tan like that her father maintained to complement his tennis whites, either. But the hard, bronzed kind.

The kind worn by a man who could drop a thug to the ground without so much as creasing the classic black tux he wore.

"Don't move." Despite the laughter and music floating on the night air from the wedding reception, his quiet voice could still be heard.

She held her breath and looked at Drago, not wanting to acknowledge her own fear of what he might do. But he subsided, sitting on the ground, glaring at her, as if the entire situation were her fault.

It probably was, of course. Most things that went wrong in the sphere Annie Hess occupied *were* her fault.

And now, she had Logan Drake—her big brother's friend—to deal with as well.

"Are you all right?"

She gingerly brushed her hands together. Her palms stung like mad. She'd been trying to get Logan's attention for the past two days, ever since he'd arrived for Will's wedding. She hadn't intended him to notice her in this manner, though.

"Annie." Logan's voice was a little sharper. "Are you all right?"

She pushed her hair out of her face and nodded. He was watching her, his expression neutral. "Go back to the house," he said evenly. "Call 911. And get your brother or your father."

Her stomach clenched. "No."

Logan raised his eyebrows. "No?"

Drago smirked with satisfaction.

Annie wanted to kick herself. She'd been working like a dog to convince Drago that their relationship was over, that she didn't care what happened to him as long as he left her alone. "I don't want to cause a scene at Will's wedding," she said.

His gaze drifted over her and she shivered. "Then you shouldn't have invited your boyfriend, here."

"I didn't." She eyed Drago. He'd been the last person she'd wanted to see. And though she'd threatened him with the combined wrath of her father and brother, she'd failed to get rid of him on her own. "And he's not my boyfriend."

Logan's lip curled. "Right."

"Ah, baby doll, don't lie to the dude."

"Shut up, Drago." She wasn't going to sit there on the ground like a schoolgirl beneath Logan's censorious look. But rising was hardly an easy task, given the tight fit of her thigh-length dress. And she'd be damned if she'd hike the thing up to her hips just to stand.

Not with the way Drago was leering at her. She was nearly positive he was high. Why else would he have been so intent on getting her alone? Despite the appearance she'd fostered to others, he'd known the terms of their deal, and it hadn't included *her*.

Logan finally made an impatient sound and reached down, sliding his hands under her arms and lifting her to her feet as if she were some toddler who couldn't find her balance on her own. But when his hands slid away from her again, her heart thudded and her skin prickled in an entirely adult way.

His gaze traveled downward from her face, and it took every speck of nonchalance she possessed not to shiver visibly.

Logan Drake was her brother's friend. He was also her best friend's older brother. Yet she could probably count on her hand the number of times she'd actually *seen* him, and those incidents had left their impression. This time was no exception. He was dressed in the same sedate black tux that all the groomsmen wore, yet Logan possessed an edge the others did not.

And there was nothing Annie Hess liked better than walking on the edge.

"Get out of here, Drago, or I really will turn you in to the cops, myself." She didn't look away from Logan as she spoke. She'd warned Drago that she'd turn him in, that she'd sic her father, the venerable judge George Hess, on him if he continued bugging her. He didn't need to know what an empty threat it was. She'd already sought out her father—and her mother—during the reception, when she'd realized Drago wasn't going to be so easily shaken.

Neither George nor Lucia—that's Loo-sha, dear—had been remotely interested in setting aside their champagne or their friends' company to assist their wayward daughter.

Again, her own fault. She'd taken up with Drago in the first place to annoy her parents. But that was before she'd realized he was into a whole scene she wanted no part of.

Annie walked the wild edge, but she wasn't a fool, and she had no desire to acquaint herself with a jail cell; which was definitely where Drago was headed if Will's warnings were to be believed. Since her brother was already ensconced in the prosecutor's office, believing him wasn't difficult.

"You're not going to turn me in, baby doll." Drago rose, flipping back his shock of gold-brown hair. He smiled, as cocky as he'd ever been. "You and me are two of a kind, remember?"

That uneasiness she didn't want to acknowledge coiled in her stomach again. "Hardly."

"Annie, go and do what I said." Logan's voice was inflexible.

She looked from him to Drago. Going to her father would be useless. And Will—well, Will was already annoyed with her. They'd always been a team. But now her brother had married the dazzling Noelle and Annie's one claim to any semblance of family who mattered was gone. He'd chosen Noelle, and that was that. Just like Lucia had warned. Will would have a new life and the troublesome Annie would have no place in it. He had a golden career ahead of him with Noelle-the-perfect right beside him. "Fine," she bluffed, and headed up the walkway. Her painfully high heels clicked on the stone.

The last place she wanted to go was back into the fray of the reception. Yet, if she hadn't cut off her own nose to spite her face and flatly refused to be one of Noelle's bridesmaids, Annie would be dressed in elegantly tasteful salmon silk and standing up there with the rest of the wedding party while Will and Noelle shoved raspberry-cream-filled wedding cake into one another's mouths and Drago wouldn't have had an opportunity to get near her.

"All right, all right. I'm going."

She stopped and looked back. Drago was shaking his head, backing away from Logan.

"Stay away from Annie. Permanently," Logan said. Her heart stuttered.

Drago's lips curled. "Wanting a little jailbait yourself?"

Annie winced as Logan's fist shot out, clipping Drago's jaw. Drago stumbled back, but didn't go down. His smile was oily as he turned and jogged away, disappearing into the thick stand of trees that bordered the palatial Hess estate.

Logan looked ready to pursue him and Annie hastily darted back to him, grabbing his arm. "He's an idiot. Let him go."

"So he can get away with assaulting you?"

"He didn't—" She exhaled. The truth was, she wasn't entirely sure what Drago would have done if Logan hadn't come along when he had. Before now, Drago had seemed content with the bargain they'd struck—she'd get him an in at her private school so he could pick up mechanic work on all the rich kids' cars, and though in public he'd portray the totally inappropriate boyfriend, in private he'd keep his hands off her. "Look, I'm glad you came when you did. But I meant it when I said I didn't want to cause a scene during the reception."

"I don't think you've ever walked away from creating a scene. What did your parents do? Threaten to disown you if something happened today?"

"My parents threaten to disown me every other week," she assured blandly. The truth was, she hadn't wanted to disappoint Will any more than she already had with her refusal to accept Noelle's efforts at friendship. "Believe me, they'll probably be disappointed when the day ends without me doing something to embarrass them in front of their guests."

From the other side of the boathouse, where the

enormous awning had been erected on the richly groomed grounds, applause and cheering broke out from the revelers.

"Is that why you wouldn't go ask for their help?"

Annie kept her smile in place, but it took an effort. "As it happens, I did ask."

He drew his eyebrows together. "And?"

She shrugged. "Well, Drago didn't leave until just now, did he?" She didn't like the look in his eyes. The one that seemed a little too close to pitying. "You should be back there." She tilted her head in the direction of the party. "Will's probably tossing the garter or something about now."

"Why aren't *you* back there?"

"What? To catch the bouquet?" She managed an uncaring shrug. "Not my style."

His eyebrow lifted. "You're seventeen years old. You don't have a style yet."

She nearly laughed. "I'll be eighteen in a few months, and you know better than that. Annie's style is to go wherever there is trouble, and if there isn't trouble yet, there soon will be once she arrives."

"Is that what you really think or are you just quoting your parents?"

Her smile faltered a little. "What's the difference?"

Another burst of clapping and laughter sprang through the night. Logan's steady, silent look made her feel positively itchy. "If you don't like something, Annie, you're the one who has the power to change it."

"Annie'll never change," she assured. "My parents say that all the time." She hated the way her throat felt, all tight. She focused hard on the empty champagne bottle lying in the grass beside the walkway until her vision cleared.

Then she nudged the bottle with the pointed toe of her red pump. "Pity about the champagne. It spilled out when I tried to hit Drago with the bottle. Such a waste."

"I think you've already had plenty."

"Me? I'm underage, Logan, remember? You don't think I meant to drink it myself, do you?"

The corner of his lips tilted. "I'm well aware of your age, and yes, I do think you meant to drink it." His voice was as dry as the imported bubbly.

The man was intoxicating. More so than any amount of champagne she might have consumed on the sly.

"That's why you snuck down here by the boathouse, I suspect. To drink your little heart out."

"How nice of you to notice." She'd perfected that bored tone when she was knee-high to a grasshopper. But, when she languidly brushed her hair back from her shoulder and his gaze tracked the movement, she hid another little shudder.

"Oh, you're noticeable, all right. Somebody should put you on a leash."

Despite his wholly overwhelming appeal, she was more comfortable with this sort of exchange with him than any other. She didn't want his pity. She wanted his hands on her. Simple.

Her lips curved. "Why, Logan. Is there a bit of kink hiding beneath your straight-arrow exterior?"

He didn't look amused.

She exhaled, pouting a little, and walked closer to him. Her heels were so ungodly high that the top of her head nearly reached his chin. She tilted her head back a little, leaning toward him. Her heart was beating so hard that she wondered hazily if he could see it right through the wedge of skin revealed by the plunging V of her dress.

"What the hell do you think you're doing?"

"Giving you a proper thank you." She pressed her lips to his jaw, settling her hand against his chest when her knees seemed too shaky to hold her.

"Fine." His voice was clipped. "You're welcome."

He hadn't moved, and she felt the heady beat of his heart right through the shirt he wore. Her palm still hurt, but the white silk felt unreasonably soft as she moved her hand down over his hard abdomen. Her lips tingled as she drew them along the hard, raspy line of his jaw. She rose on her toes, her mouth slowly, agonizingly nearing his. For an altogether too brief moment, his hand slid behind her neck, tangling in her hair. His lips hovered enticingly close to hers.

Then he suddenly set her from him, dragging her hand away from his belt as he pushed her back. "Dammit, Annie. You don't have to behave this way, just for the sake of getting some attention from your worthless parents."

Her defenses closed around her again like a vise. "You want me, Logan. I know you do." She leaned toward him once more.

His hands held her off. "Grow up." His voice was hard. "You're a beautiful, selfish little girl who doesn't think about anything other than what she wants."

His words stung. Not because it was the first time she'd heard such accusations, but because they came from *him.* "And you're saying you don't want to kiss me? Touch me? Believe me, Logan, I know when a guy's interested.'' Her gaze ran over him.

''Is this what you do back at that expensive boarding school you and my sister go to? Convince yourself that any guy you throw yourself at is interested just because you've gotten a physical reaction out of him?''

The truth was, she hadn't thrown herself at *any* man, until now. Everything up to then—the scores of boyfriends, Drago, the alcohol, the failed tests—had been just a front. A futile attempt to get kicked out of a school she'd loathed every minute of the three years she'd been there, to go back to parents who didn't have time or interest in her, anyway. The only reason she'd been allowed home from Bendlemaier now was because of Will's wedding.

''Don't worry about Sara,'' she said smoothly. Her roommate was at the exclusive school on scholarship, and despite the differences between them, they'd become good friends. ''Your sister's still as pure as the driven snow,'' Annie went on. ''And in a few short months, we'll graduate from that godforsaken prison and be out of there altogether.'' She smiled. ''I'll be eighteen and you'll be, what? Twenty-three? Twenty-four? Come on, Logan. It's only a few months away. Weeks, really. Don't be so uptight.''

His eyes narrowed. ''So what do you propose here, Annie? Go into the boathouse? We'll just pull that excuse for a dress you're wearing up another three inches and go at it, just because you think I *want* you? You're my friend's kid sister and I don't care what you think I do or don't want. If you want to get laid, go find that sleaze, Drago. He's probably still hiding out there in the woods. I'm not interested.''

Without a second glance, he strode up the walk.

Annie leaned back against the stucco again, his words ringing in her head. There was truth in Logan's words. She *was* selfish. She wanted what she wanted when she wanted it.

She looked out over the narrow gleam of water beyond the end of the dock. More laughter and cheering echoed on the night air.

If it hadn't been for Logan, who knew what Drago might have done? Logan was the only one who'd noticed her absence, the only one who'd thought to investigate, and he didn't even like her.

It was pathetic.

She should have just stayed at Bendlemaier.

She swallowed past the knot in her throat and pushed away from the boathouse. She kicked off her shoes and they disappeared into the night to land silently somewhere in the thick green grass.

Then she walked around to the front of the boathouse and went inside where the catering crew had stored the cases of champagne.

Nobody would miss another bottle.

Chapter One

There was no mistaking the sound of breaking glass.

Annie closed her eyes at the latest shatter and ordered her nerves to stop jumping all over the place. She didn't even really need to open her eyes to move to the rear portion of the shop, though she did. She knew every corner, every surface, inside and out. But considering how edgy she'd been for the past two days, it wouldn't have surprised her greatly if she *did* run into one of the chrome-and-glass display racks as she moved.

She stepped through the doorway that separated the stock- and workroom from the retail front of Island Botanica and took in the scene with a glance.

Bunches of lavender, rosemary and California poppy hung drying from the large grid-shaped rack suspended from the ceiling. And below the colorful, fragrant display a teenaged girl stood in the midst of broken dark-green glassware. "Are you hurt?"

Her niece looked down at the mess around her heavy leather boots. "That's the third bottle I've broken." Riley's voice sounded thick, as if she were near tears.

There were no signs of blood and Annie's heart began to settle again. She shrugged and plucked the broom from the hook on the wall and began sweeping up the shards. "It happens," she said calmly. "Particularly with a concrete floor." She realized her hands were trembling and tightened them around the broom handle. "Sara and I have joked about having the floor in here padded with foam because we've broken so many things." She smiled a little. "Too impractical. At least concrete's easy to sweep."

The dozen bracelets around Riley's slender wrist jangled as she tucked her waving blond hair behind her ears. She stepped out of the way as Annie swept. "Dad'll pay for whatever I damage."

Annie's heart clutched a little at that. Since she'd unexpectedly shown up on Annie's doorstep two days ago, Riley had not voluntarily mentioned either one of her parents. Annie had been the one to insist on calling Will and Noelle to let them know their daughter was safe.

As safe as she could be given that she was in Annie's company.

She stopped sweeping for a moment. Started to reach out and touch Riley's arm, but stopped.

Instead, she bent over the dustpan and swept the broken glass into it. Riley hadn't been thrilled when Annie had insisted on calling her parents, but she hadn't bolted, at least. "Don't be silly. Nobody has to pay for anything."

"Except you and Sara, cause now you can't sell that." The girl jerked her chin at the rain of glass that tumbled from the dustpan when Annie tipped it over the large garbage can. "Dad said you guys are barely keeping your heads above water."

"Well, a broken bottle or two isn't going to ruin us," she said dryly. "It's all right, Riley. Truly." She began sweeping over the floor once more for good measure. "Why don't you finish unpacking that crate of bottles and then we'll break for lunch."

Riley's blue gaze flicked above Annie's head and she knew the girl was looking at the plain round clock on the wall. "A little early for lunch, isn't it?"

Annie shook the dustpan over the garbage can again before putting it and the broom back. "One of the perks of being an owner. Lunch whenever we want. I'll take you over to Maisy's Place. The cook there does a great lunch, and maybe we can still sit outside if the rain holds off." She managed a smile, feeling lighter at the prospect. Trying to keep Riley occupied in the shop all morning had been harder than she'd expected. But the shop needed tending, even on a stormy day, and she hadn't wanted to leave Riley alone. "Let me know when you're finished with that crate."

Threat of tears apparently gone, Riley nodded and reached again into the packing material that surrounded each bottle in the wooden crate. After a moment, Annie made herself go back out to the front of the shop. Riley didn't need her looking over her shoulder.

It was quiet that morning, much as she'd expect it to be in the middle of the week. Turnabout's small tourist trade picked up around the weekends, and the herbal shop, Island Botanica, Annie owned with her friend Sara Drake, picked up business then as a result.

Thank goodness for their mail-order trade, she thought faintly. If not for that exceptionally successful portion of their business, Will's opinion would have been borne out, and there would probably be no shop at all. Which was an unbearable thought.

She picked up a dusting cloth and moved across the light pine floor to the display cases at the window. The shop was small but still had an airy, simple and clean feel to it that Annie loved as much now as she had when she and Sara had opened it five years earlier.

Sitting atop the clear glass shelves were their trademark green glass bottles, jars and matching tubes. A person could get almost everything from tonics to perfume at Island Botanica, and all of it was made right there on Turnabout Island. She turned a bottle so the silver print on the narrow ivory label could be seen more clearly and dashed her rag over a fingerprint smudging the shelf.

She glanced through the windows lining the front of the shop, glad to see the sidewalk was still dry, then looked up at the dark clouds in the sky. If it hadn't been the middle of the week, she suspected that the threatening weather would have chased off any prospective customers, anyway. There was a storm moving in, no doubt about it.

Turnabout Island often had drizzly days, and the climate was ideal for the fertile fields that supplied the shop. But it wasn't all that often they had such threatening clouds hovering overhead as they'd had for the past several days.

The clouds had rolled in the same day Riley had arrived. Annie had been a mess of nerves, dread and euphoria ever since. Her niece had run away from home, but instead of disappearing completely, she'd come to Annie.

Annie still didn't really know why.

She twisted the cloth in her hands, turning toward the door as she heard the soft, tinkling bell that signaled someone entering. Her gaze had barely caught a glimpse of height and gleaming brown hair when Riley came in from the back.

"Auntie Annie, I'm finished with the—" Riley's voice stopped cold.

Annie glanced at her. "Great, Riley. Thanks. Just sit tight for a minute while I take care of—" Her own voice broke off at the sight of their visitor. Her foot fell back a step and she bumped into one of the display cases after all. Bottles jangled ominously but she was so rooted in shock she didn't even reach back to steady them. "Logan?"

"I warned them," her niece said, lips tight. "I *warned* them not to come after me. So he sent *you* instead. I'm not stupid, you know. I recognize you from Mom and Dad's wedding pictures."

The man drew his eyebrows together as he continued watching Riley. "Excuse me?"

Riley didn't lose her mutinous expression.

Annie felt as though her jaw must be near the floor as she gaped at the incomer. "Logan," she said again. "Logan *Drake?*" It had been years since she'd seen him in the flesh. *Years.* She'd believed that he'd lost touch with Will shortly after Will and Noelle got married. And even though Sara had spoken of him from time to time, the sight of him was still like a flashback to another life. Another time.

Another Annie.

Finally, the man looked from Riley to her. "Hey, Annie." The corner of his lips tilted and a fine spray of lines crinkled out from the corners of his unforgettably blue, thickly-lashed eyes. "It's been a long time."

Annie's stomach dipped and swayed. She wasn't sure who unnerved her more. Riley or Logan, who clearly wasn't surprised to see *her*. "A long time," she agreed faintly.

"You're a friend of my dad's," Riley accused.

"Who's your dad?"

Riley crossed her arms and stuck out her chin.

Annie started to push back her hair, realized she was still holding the dust cloth, and dropped it on the counter next to the cash register. "Logan—" even saying his name aloud felt odd "—this is m-my niece, Riley."

"Will's daughter?" Logan looked at the teen again. Assessing. "No kidding. Is he on the island, too?"

Riley rolled her eyes.

"No." Annie quickly stepped closer to her niece. She didn't entirely trust that Riley wouldn't bolt. And though Annie knew the girl couldn't get to the mainland from the island as easily as a person could hop a bus out of an ordinary town, she didn't want to take any chances. She wanted Riley to go home, not run away again somewhere she couldn't be found at all.

"He and Noelle still live in Washington state," she told him.

Then she looked at Riley, speaking quickly before whatever was forming on her niece's lips could emerge. "This is Logan Drake. He might be an old friend of your dad's, but he's also Sara's *brother*. I...I'm sure he's here to see her and Dr. Hugo. He's from Turnabout. Isn't that right, Logan?"

His half smile didn't waver. "I grew up here," he confirmed.

"Bet you couldn't wait to leave it. There's hardly anything to do here, you know, even if it *is* part of California. There's, like, only five cars on the entire island. It's boring as hell."

"Riley!" She sent Logan an awkward smile. It was true that Turnabout was not a large island. Situated well off the coast of California, it was barely eleven miles long and less than half that wide, with a single road almost exactly bisecting the island down the length. Annie didn't own a car. Most people on the island didn't and instead walked, rode bicycles, or occasionally zipped around in golf carts.

"Sara's in San Diego for the week, I'm afraid," Annie finally said. "She, uh, she didn't say she was expecting you home." Truth be told, Sara rarely talked about Logan anymore, and when she did it was to speculate over the source of the money he seemed to have—evidenced by the generous checks he'd occasionally send Sara's way—or, more commonly, to bemoan his long absence.

That half smile of his, little more than a quirk at the corner of his lips really, hadn't moved. For some reason, it made her uncommonly nervous.

"She didn't know I was coming to visit," he said.

She understood his clarification. He wasn't *home*. He had no intention of staying. Though why he felt the need to clarify himself escaped her. It wasn't as if he was there to see her. She knew good and well what his opinion had been of her. There were some things that were not in her memory banks from sixteen years ago, but his opinion of her wasn't one of them.

Before she could stop the nervous gesture, she'd run her fingers through her hair. "Well, like I said, Sara is away. Riley and I were just heading over to Maisy's Place for lunch. You're welcome to join us."

He looked at her thoughtfully and she swallowed. What was she doing? She didn't ask men out to lunch, or to anything else, for that matter. Not anymore. Not even one on whom she'd once had an unrequited crush the size of the Cascade Mountains. Not even one who was the brother of her best friend.

"Oh." Her brain belatedly kicked into gear with an explanation for that look of his. "Of course you'll be wanting to see your dad, probably. I saw Dr. Hugo this morning when we came in to the shop. His office— well, of course you'd know where his office is." She was babbling and felt like an idiot.

"Actually, lunch sounds good."

For a moment, her heart seemed to stop beating. It had always been like that when Logan was around. Even back when she was only seventeen years old to his twenty-three. "Okay," she said faintly.

Riley huffed, a sound halfway between a snort and a groan. Annie ignored it. She was only Riley's aunt; pretending that she had a right to correct the girl's atrocious manners was—

She broke off the thought, recognizing the words that had been silently streaking through her mind. Words that Lucia had used, too often, to describe Annie's behavior, Annie's attitude, Annie's habits.

Nothing Riley did was *atrocious,* she reminded herself. The girl was a teenager, troubled enough to seek out an aunt she barely knew. The only thing Annie could do for her was to convince her voluntarily to go back home to her parents. As quickly as possible. Considering Riley's statement just now that the island was boring, perhaps she should focus on that angle with the girl—

She realized both Riley and Logan were staring at her. Obviously waiting. Probably wondering what was wrong with her. She smiled weakly. "Right. Lunch." She hurried into the back to get her wallet and grabbed the shop door keys as she came back out.

Logan and Riley were watching each other. It was a toss-up who looked more wary of the other. And now, because of her big mouth, they'd get to sit at a lunch table together. Joy, oh joy. She reached for the door only to find Logan's hand beating her to it. She jumped a little and felt her face flush at the nervous reaction.

Riley glared at her.

Logan looked satanically amused.

She hurriedly locked the door and set off across the bumpy road. What she wouldn't give for some of the mindless bravado she'd once had. She would have had a response for Riley's smart-aleck attitude, and she'd have looked Logan right back in those ungodly blue eyes of his without having some desire to collapse in a puddle.

She sneaked a look over her shoulder at him.

He looked right at her. Her heart squeezed and she hurriedly looked forward again. Who was she kidding? Even at seventeen, *particularly* at seventeen, she'd been a puddle where he was concerned.

Riley was already nearly Annie's own height. She easily caught up with her. "I don't care whose brother he is," she whispered, not altogether quietly. "I'll bet you a million bucks that my dad sent him to drag me home." A low roll of thunder underscored her words.

Annie looked up at the sky, half expecting lightning to strike right down from the roiling black clouds to the earth at her feet. Such an event would have been about as ordinary as having Riley and then Logan show up on Turnabout. She was acutely aware of the occasional scrape of his boot on the road as he walked right behind them.

She shivered. "You don't have a million dollars."

Riley made that impatient sound again.

"Well, maybe he is here because of your dad," she acknowledged softly. Coincidences did happen in life, but for him to show up now? It was stretching it.

"I won't go," Riley said flatly.

Yes, you will, Annie answered silently. Thunder rolled again. The air seemed far too still and full of energy, lying in wait for some perfect moment to flash.

"Storm coming," Logan said behind them.

Annie quickened her step, heading down the road to Maisy Fielding's inn. As far as she was concerned, the storm had already arrived.

Chapter Two

"As I live and breathe. Is that my very own nephew, Logan Drake?" Maisy Fielding, all five-feet-nothing of her, stood in the middle of the entry to Maisy's Place, her hands on her hips.

Despite himself, Logan felt amusement tug at his lips. Maisy Fielding was an aunt of sorts—her deceased husband having been his mom's cousin—and she looked the same as she had the last time he'd seen her. The same corkscrew red curls, the same migraine-inspiring colorful clothes, the same hefty attitude screaming from the pores of her diminutive person. "That's what my driver's license says."

She laughed heartily, then tugged his shoulders until he had to bend over her. She wrapped her skinny arms around him for a surprisingly strong hug. "Still have a smart mouth, I see," she said, patting his back.

"Running away from Turnabout didn't change that a lick." She let go of him, and peered up into his face, her expression shrewd.

He wondered what she saw. Whatever it was, she waved her arm toward one side after a moment, encompassing the lush landscaping that surrounded the main inn. "Surprised you haven't managed to lose your license somewhere along the way. It took nearly ten years for the trees over at the corner to recover after you plowed that darned fool car of yours into them."

Behind him, Logan heard Riley stifle a snort. Of laughter or disgust, he couldn't tell. "Didn't expect the brakes to go out, Maisy," he said easily. "I managed not to take out the side of the inn at least."

She laughed again, a sure sign that time could heal some wounds. Twenty-three years ago when he'd been a brand-new sixteen-year-old behind the wheel of a rattletrap car his father had forbidden him to buy, Maisy had been plenty mad about him mowing down her trees. She'd meted out her punishment over an entire summer of drudgery. He'd done everything from scraping paint off her kitchen cabinets to babysitting her precocious daughter. Back then, he'd preferred dealing with the paint to dealing with Tessa. She'd been a pain in the ass.

And he still felt badly that he hadn't been around years later when she'd died. He'd only learned the news from Sara when one of her scarce letters had caught up to him.

"Well, if you're here for lunch, come on in," Maisy said, her eyes taking in Annie and Riley as well. If she saw anything unusual in Logan accompanying them, she kept it to herself, and Logan was glad. Maisy wasn't known for keeping her mouth shut when she figured something was her business. "Grapevine must have a branch missing that I didn't hear about you before seeing you." She turned toward the building. "Hugo didn't mention a word that you were coming."

Logan held open the door for the females, ignoring Maisy's reference to his father. "Business must be good. I remember you used to offer only breakfast."

"More tourists coming to Turnabout. They needed to eat somewhere." She walked straight through to an open-air dining area where at least two dozen other people were already seated at the round tables dotting the saltillo-tiled floor. "Sit anywhere you like. If it starts to rain, I'll find you a spot inside. Somewhere." She patted Logan's arm and scurried back inside.

"Have a preference?" He looked at Riley, who ignored him, and Annie, who shook her head slightly. He headed to the table farthest from the other patrons. Seeing Maisy was one thing, but he had no particular desire to run into anyone else he might know. He was only there to clear his conscience, not renew old acquaintances.

He held out Annie's seat, then habit had him sitting with his back to what passed for a wall in the dining area—a redwood trellis congested with climbing bougainvillea. A teenaged waitress he didn't recognize brought them glasses of water with lemon slices in them and they ordered after she'd recited the day's menu.

When she was gone, silence settled, broken only by the murmur of voices from the other diners. Logan looked around. The middle-aged couple with sunburned faces and crispy-new vacation clothes at the table nearest them were having a softly hissed argument. To their right was a smaller table, occupied by a lone young woman. She was reading a paperback book, occasionally looking up and studying the other diners as she toyed with her soup bowl. It was obvious to Logan that she was more interested in the people around her than the contents of her bowl. Beyond her was a young couple. Honeymooners, if he was any judge. They couldn't keep their hands apart long enough to eat their sandwiches, and beneath the iron and glass table, the woman was running her toes up and down the man's ankle. Logan half expected to see her slide over into her partner's lap.

He looked back at Annie. She was sitting quietly, her expression closed. Riley was studying her fingernails—painted such an ungodly black that it looked as if her hands had been caught beneath a ton of bricks.

The school picture that Will had shown him the day before had indicated how much she took after him, but in person the resemblance seemed less marked. Her expression tightened when she noticed him looking at her and she shifted in her chair, crossing her arms.

Classic defensiveness.

"I guess I don't need to ask if you and Sara kept in touch after you two graduated from Bendlemaier." Logan turned his attention back to Annie. He was perfectly aware of Riley's increased defensiveness when he mentioned the school. Another thing that Will had clued him into.

He and Noelle wanted to send their daughter to the exclusive boarding school. But it was apparent that Riley liked the idea even less than Annie once had.

Annie's smile looked forced. "I, um, I didn't graduate from Bendlemaier. But we kept in touch when she went off to college. We'd talked often enough about wanting our own shop, and when the opportunity arose, we went for it."

For some reason, Logan had assumed Annie had been in college with Sara. Showed how much he knew about his sister. He wondered if Sara had changed as much as Annie. Even though it hadn't been in his plans—which were to do what needed doing and get out of there as quickly as possible—he had more than a fleeting desire to see his kid sister.

He'd talked to her a few times in the past ten years on the phone, but he hadn't seen her in person in longer than that. He still remembered her expression the last time they'd seen each other. Confused. Hurt. It had felt like his skin was being peeled away to know he'd never come back to Turnabout to be any sort of brother that mattered. Instead, he called when the need to do so grew too great and sent her money to salve his conscience. After enough years, he could almost convince himself his system worked.

But he wasn't there to deal with *his* family issues. So he studied Annie for a moment. He'd fully expected to see her, since Will had told him that his daughter was staying with her, but he hadn't expected any of the feelings that had hit him when he did. "Your hair used to be longer, didn't it?" He knew good and well how long it had been. Thick and shining, its wild white-blond curls had reached down to the small of her back. All those years ago, she'd used that mane like a weapon against any male in her vicinity.

"Yes." She poked her fork into her water glass,

spearing the lemon, which she squeezed back into the water. Her cheeks looked vaguely red. "You look pretty much the same to me." She glanced at Riley, making him wonder what she was thinking. "A little older, but aren't we all?"

"All this reminiscing makes me want to gag."

"Then face the other way before you do, Riley, so you don't ruin our lunches," Logan suggested mildly.

She glared at him. It made him want to smile. She was very much like her aunt had once been. Full of attitude. The style of clothing had changed some in the past decade and a half, but she wore hers just as tightly and flauntingly as Annie had ever done.

He watched Annie's down-turned head for a moment. There was nothing flaunting about Annie's appearance, now. She had on a sleeveless khaki jumper that nearly reached her ankles over a short-sleeved white T-shirt. The dress was shapeless and the neckline of the shirt didn't even reveal the base of her slender throat.

She wore a plain watch with a thin black band on her left wrist and no other visible jewelry. Gone were the jangling metal bracelets, the chains around her neck, the multiple sets of dangling earrings. Her brown lashes looked soft and naked and if she wore a hint of makeup, she'd done it too subtly for him to tell. When she'd been seventeen she'd seemed to pile on the stuff with a trowel.

"Geez. Take a picture, why don't you?" Riley rolled her eyes and shook her head at him, her disgust obvious.

Annie looked up, her gaze flicking from her niece to Logan's face. Then her cheeks flushed again. She moistened her lips and seemed about to say something, but the waitress returned, arms laden with their orders, leaving Logan to wonder what had caused that flush— if it had to do with the past.

She'd never seemed the blushing type before.

The last time he'd seen her had been at her parent's palatial Seattle home, where he, along with the rest of the wedding party, had spent the night following Will's wedding. He'd been pretty damned angry with her.

But even angrier with himself. Her youth could explain her actions. He'd had no such excuse.

"Pass the ketchup, please."

He handed Riley the bottle, vaguely surprised by her politeness. But then again, attitude or not, she *was* Will and Noelle's daughter. He watched her dump it over her French fries. "Like to have one French fry with your ketchup?"

She made a face then nodded. He took the bottle when she was finished, doing the same thing with his own plate. "Me, too."

It earned him a studiously bored look.

Annie had ordered a salad. She stabbed her fork into it, moving lettuce and chunky vegetables from side to side, but not seeming to eat any of it.

"So, what did happen when you left Bendlemaier?"

She didn't look up from her salad. "Not a lot."

"How come you don't still live on Turnabout, if you came from here?" Riley dredged a fry back and forth through her pool of ketchup.

"I had a job that took me elsewhere." It was true enough, though hardly the entire truth. He had the sense that Riley had only posed the question to keep him from asking more questions of his own to her aunt. It struck him as oddly protective.

"What kinda job?"

"Riley, it's none of our business."

He shook his head at Annie's protest. "I became a spy."

"Yeah, right." Riley rolled her eyes and scooped up her dripping French fry, licking her fingers afterward.

"Okay, I'm a consultant," he said dryly. The lie had always been more palatable for people than the truth—even if he'd dared to share the truth with anybody who mattered. Even his associates had a hard time stomaching it. There were a lot of agents who worked for Coleman Black, the head of Hollins-Winword, in many capacities. But there was need for only one clean-up man.

"Consultant for what? Who?"

"Did you pick up that questioning technique from your dad? I always figured if he hadn't wanted to be a lawyer, he'd have made a good cop."

The teen wasn't fooled. "That's not an answer."

"What happened with *your* law degree?" Annie finally spoke.

"I stuck it in a closet where it's gathered a lot of dust." He smiled grimly. He did practice law. Just in a manner most people didn't want to be aware of. He'd felt that way himself many times. Until recently, though, he'd always been able to shake it, and get on with the job at hand.

A young woman with a white towel wrapped around her hips stopped by their table. "Anything else I can bring you?"

Logan shook his head. Riley sat back, her arms crossed. She'd eaten her ketchup-drenched fries and half her hamburger. Annie—who hadn't eaten even half of the salad, smiled up at the waitress. "I think we're fine, Janie. Thanks."

The waitress moved away. She hadn't been the one to serve them their meal.

"Who's the girl?" he asked, watching after her. "She looks familiar."

Annie followed his gaze toward the departing waitress. "Janie Vega. She helps Maisy out when things are busy. She's actually a stained-glass artist, though. Has her own studio on the island."

"Vega?"

Annie nodded. "I suppose you knew Sam Vega? She's his younger sister."

"I went to school with Sam." Janie had been a baby back then.

"He's sheriff now."

Logan shook his head, truly surprised at that. "When we were young, Sam wanted off the island worse than I did."

Annie toyed with her water glass. "When Sara said she hardly ever heard from you she wasn't joking. Otherwise you'd have known he was the sheriff."

Riley huffed again. "This is too old for words. I'm outta here."

"Where are you going?"

"I'll go back to your house or something."

Logan watched Annie's face. A dozen expressions seemed to cross it. Everything from alarm to reluctance to resignation. She passed her keys to her niece. "You can watch the shop until I get there."

Riley slowly took the keys. "You trust me?"

"You're not planning to go anywhere else, are you?"

Anywhere else like running away again, Logan interpreted.

"No." She turned on her heel and strode out of the dining area. Logan watched her go, calculating how likely it would be for her to get off the island if she'd been set on doing so. He'd already talked to Diego Montoya who—as he'd suspected—still ran the only ferry on the island, only to learn the old man was already on the watch for Riley Hess. If the girl were to try to leave, she wouldn't be able to do so on Diego's boat. And fortunately for Logan's current purposes, the other residents of the island seemed to have held to the strange tradition of not owning any kind of watercraft more sophisticated than a dinghy. Only a fool would attempt the crossing in that small a craft.

When Riley was gone, Logan looked back to find Annie watching him. She set down her fork and pushed aside the salad with an air of finality. Her expression was unreadable. "Riley was right. Will *did* send you. I wasn't aware that you two were even in touch anymore."

"I was in Olympia and happened to look him up. He told me Riley had run away."

She raised her eyebrows. "*Happened?* Quite a coincidence. And how perfectly convenient that your consulting job allows you to head off to little-known islands whenever it suits you."

"I'm between assignments right now." It wasn't often he found himself feeling defensive, and he'd be damned if he knew why he did now. His answer was true enough, though. Except he didn't know how he could stomach another assignment after the last FU-BAR. He'd told Cole that he'd needed a break, which was how Logan came to be helping out on what should have been a straightforward runaway case. Except that Will hadn't been the one to ask him to help out. It had been Cole. Turns out his boss and Will had some dealings with each other. Dealings he hadn't known about until now.

Despite that, however, Logan didn't necessarily trust his boss to leave Logan to his task if his particular talents suddenly became necessary again. Cole's priorities were simple. Hollins-Winword—and all that it stood for, all that it protected—came first.

Annie's lips were pressed together. "Your job—whatever it is—doesn't really matter, anyway. Will should have come after Riley himself."

Logan didn't necessarily disagree. Another argument he'd had with Cole and Will. "Your brother didn't want Riley doing something even more drastic."

"She threatened to run again if he came after her."

"I heard."

"But she needs to go home."

The fine line of her jaw looked tight. In fact, everything about Annie looked tight. *Up*tight. It wasn't a demeanor he'd have expected her to wear. "Is she causing you difficulties?"

"No. No, of course she isn't." She looked like she wanted to say more, but didn't.

"Has she told you why she left home?"

"Riley doesn't confide in me."

He frowned. "Come on, Annie. Riley didn't just run away and disappear. Fortunately. She came to *you*."

Annie shook her head. She fiddled with her fork and spoon, neatly aligning them. "She's just curious about her black-sheep aunt who is odd enough to live on a small island."

Black sheep? She currently looked more like Bo-Peep to him. "Will and Noelle want to send Riley to Bendlemaier."

"It's a fine school."

Logan watched her for a long moment. "You hated it there."

"The academic program is—"

"You called it a prison."

"—unparalleled. Riley is very—"

"You did everything you could to get out of there."

"—bright. She'll excel there."

"Obviously you succeeded in getting out, since you've admitted you didn't graduate from Bendlemaier." He recognized her face. But the resemblance to the Annie of old was nil. "That's probably what your parents said when they sent you there. That you'd excel."

She stiffened. "You never did think much of me, Logan. But are you *really* comparing me to George and Lucia Hess?"

Impatience rolled through him. He leaned toward her across the small round table. "What the hell's happened to you, Annie?"

"I grew up," she said evenly. "What happened to you? You're the one who pretty much disappeared after Will and Noelle's wedding."

If she knew, she'd keep him miles away from Riley. "This isn't about me."

"Nor is it about me. This is about Riley and the fact that you're here to take her home because her father, my brother, couldn't be bothered to come after her himself."

"You know his reasons. He and Noelle are being cautious, given what Riley has threatened."

"Do you really think that Riley doesn't want her parents' attention despite what she says to the contrary?" She sat back, seeming to realize that her voice had risen. "Okay, so fine. You're doing your old friend a favor by retrieving his daughter. Actually, I'm surprised Will waited even a day to retrieve her, considering the unhealthy influence I'm bound to have on her."

Her tone was even. Neither defensive nor sarcastic, but factual. She could have been reciting geographic statistics from an encyclopedia for all the emotion she showed.

It bugged the hell out of him.

Years ago, there had probably been a portrait of Annie in the dictionary beside the word *precocious,* but she hadn't been a danger to anyone other than herself. "How long has it been since you've seen Will in person?" All Will had said during that very brief meeting they'd had—the only time they'd seen each other in more than fifteen years, in fact—was that Annie occasionally visited for Christmas, flying in and out just as quickly.

She lifted her shoulder. "Why does it matter?"

Because Logan already suspected that Will knew *this* Annie about as well as Logan did. Before he could get into that, however, he noticed someone entering the dining area.

He stiffened. Dammit.

"Maisy told me you were here," Hugo Drake said, stopping beside their table. "I had to see it with my own eyes, though. I guess they must be building igloos in hell 'bout now since you were pretty clear that particular place had to freeze over before you'd ever step foot on the island again."

He looked up at his father, a man he'd loathed for so many years he could barely remember feeling anything else for him. Hugo Drake was still a robust man, though the years had left their mark in the white hair, the fading eyes. But the old man still had an unlit cigar sticking out of the pocket on his shirt.

Annie had risen and was dropping bills on the table.

"Where are you going?" He ignored his father.

"Back to the shop."

Her gaze darted between him and Hugo. He wondered what she was thinking. And he wondered why it mattered. He didn't care who knew about his feelings where his father was concerned. The guy had made his mother's life a misery. She'd downed a bottle of pills rather than stay married to him. Rather than hang around to finish raising her son and daughter.

Logan hadn't hated living on Turnabout so much as he'd hated being Dr. Hugo Drake's son.

He doubted all that many things had changed in the twenty years since he'd been to Turnabout, and he knew that particular thing had changed least of all.

He stood, picked up Annie's money and handed it back to her. Right or wrong, he paid his own way in life. "I'll see you later at the shop."

Her lips parted softly. But he'd already put enough cash on the table to pay the check and was walking away.

He was on Turnabout for one specific reason. Because his boss had ordered it. And that reason didn't include playing the prodigal son to the man he held responsible for his mother's death.

Chapter Three

Logan wasn't at the shop when Annie got there. Which surprised her and relieved her—and disappointed her—though she hardly wanted to dwell on that point. Given what little she knew about him now, and what she remembered of the man she'd once briefly known, she figured he wouldn't stay away for long. He'd come to the island for a purpose. She couldn't see him not fulfilling it.

Since they wanted the same thing—Riley to return home—she decided to blame any disappointment over his absence on that aspect.

Riley, though, *was* in the shop, sitting on top of the counter by the register, blowing pink bubbles in her chewing gum and watching her boots as she swung her feet in small circles.

"Has anyone come into the shop?" Annie put her wallet back in the cupboard.

"Nope."

"Any phone calls?"

"Nope."

"Any gorillas prancing down the street wearing pink tutus?"

Riley looked up, her latest bubble deflating around her small mouth. She plucked the sticky stuff from her lips and popped the wad of gum back in her mouth. "Yup."

Annie smiled faintly. She tugged at her ear, rubbed her hands down her arms. "Riley—"

"Huh-uh." Her niece hopped off the counter. "I don't wanna talk about it. I'm not going back."

"I wasn't—okay, I was." She studied the girl. "I haven't pressed you about anything since you arrived, Riley." She hadn't known what to do. Had been nearly paralyzed from taking any actions—sensible or otherwise. But Logan's arrival had spurred something. "Maybe if you'd just give Bendlemaier a chance, you'd—"

"Like you gave it a chance? I heard you tell that old dude you didn't even stay long enough to graduate."

She almost laughed. Logan was definitely not old. He was a mouthwateringly fit man in his prime. Which was not at all what she needed to be thinking about. Ever. But Logan had always had that effect on her. Even when he was scathingly telling her to grow up. "His name is Logan, he's hardly old, and I *did* go to Bendlemaier for three years, whether I graduated from there or not. But this isn't about me."

Riley shook her head, and walked over to the display nearest the door. She picked up a bottle. Studied the label. Put it back and picked up another. "How come you never got married, Auntie Annie?" She ran the phrase together like it was one long word—antee-anee.

"Nobody ever asked me," Annie answered, lost for something more appropriate. It was the last question she might have expected.

"You think women have to wait to be asked? My mom asked dad to marry her, you know."

Annie hadn't known that. But it seemed like something Noelle would be capable of doing. She wasn't a woman to wait around for someone else to speak when there was something in her sights. Annie could appreciate that trait now, though she hadn't back then. Not when she'd believed that beautiful, accomplished Noelle Reed was marrying Will and thereby taking away the only semblance of family that Annie cared about. "No, I don't think women have to wait to be asked," she told Riley. "But as it happens, there's nobody that I've ever wanted to ask anyway." She'd have to allow herself into a relationship of some sort, first.

"Do you have a boyfriend? A lover?"

Good grief, the girl was persistent. "No. I don't sleep with men I don't love." She didn't sleep with anyone.

"Why not?"

"Logan was right. You've learned your questioning technique from Will. Do *you* have a boyfriend?" Maybe it was more than just the issue of Bendlemaier that had driven Riley to run away from home.

"No."

Relief dribbled through her.

"Mom and Dad wouldn't let me date, anyway," Riley added. "They'd just think I was out trying to have sex or something."

"Sex! You've barely turned fifteen."

"So? There's a girl in my class at school—my *real* school, not that stupid Bendleboring—who is pregnant out to here." Riley's hands stuck straight out in front of her. "It's disgusting. She's stupid. I mean, hasn't she ever heard of the pill? They sell condoms in machines in the bathrooms everywhere." She dropped her hands and worked them into the pockets of her tight jeans, casting Annie a sidelong look. "Logan'd be your boyfriend if you wanted."

"Your conversation is making me dizzy," Annie murmured. From condoms to Logan? "Logan is not here to stay, obviously, and he's not interested in me."

"He stared at you all through lunch."

Only because he couldn't figure out what had happened to the wild Annie he'd known. And she hadn't felt inclined to tell him that she'd buried her alive in an inescapable crypt. "Riley—"

"Was he your boyfriend before?"

"No!" She swallowed and lowered her voice. "He was your *dad's* friend, Riley."

Riley didn't comment on that. Merely blew another enormous bubble that popped with a soft snap when she stuck it inside her mouth and bit down on it.

Annie let out her breath, feeling as chewed-up as the deflated bubble. "What if I talk to your dad about you not going to Bendlemaier? Will you go home, then? Riley, it's the middle of the school year. You're missing classes." And unlike Annie had been, her niece was a stellar student. Another reason why her appearance on Annie's doorstep seemed so shocking.

"So, I'll go to school here."

God. "That's not what I—"

"That *is* a school we pass going into town from your house, isn't it?"

Riley knew good and well that it was. It wasn't large, but the brick building was obviously a school. "Yes, but it's for the kids who *live* here."

"You just want to get rid of me, too."

She exhaled, exasperated. "Riley, nobody wants to get rid of you. But your home is with your parents. Whatever problem there is can be worked out."

"Dad says you haven't talked to Grandma and Grandpa Hess in more 'n ten years."

Your dad talks too much, Annie said silently. "Will and Noelle are nothing like George and Lucia." Thank heavens.

"Well, why can't whatever problem you've got be worked out with *them?*"

She had no parental instincts inside her. She didn't know how to deal with a young girl who—from Noelle's reports—had been captain of last year's debate team at her school. "Riley—"

"Never mind. If you don't want me here, I'll go." She suited her words with deed and pushed out the door.

Annie followed her out. Fat drops of rain had just begun to fall. The air was redolent with the scent of an impending rainstorm—wet, dusty, earthy. She hurried across the narrow sidewalk onto the bumpy road. "That's not what I said!"

Riley looked over her shoulder, continuing to walk

away from Annie. "I just thought you'd care. But no-body cares. Not really." She looked ahead, her boots picking up the pace.

Annie's heart tore. She could actually feel the pain of it ripping through her. How many times had she felt exactly the same way? Only their situations were de-cidedly different. Her parents *hadn't* cared. Riley's did.

She swiped a raindrop from her cheek, darting after her niece, grabbing her by the shoulders. Forcing her to stop. "Everyone cares, Riley. Your parents were beside themselves with worry when I talked to them."

"Right. That's why they're pounding down the door of your beach house." Riley's eyes were stormier than the sky.

And Annie knew, for once, that her instincts had been right on the mark. Riley had run away, but, de-spite her threats, she'd expected her parents to follow after her. A show of love. A grand gesture. Something to prove she mattered to them.

Déjà vu, she thought wearily and prayed that this would be the only incident of it.

"You scared them, Riley. They believed your threats." She chose her words carefully. Not wanting to worsen the situation, which—when it came to fam-ily matters—was what Annie had generally done ex-ceptionally well. "But make no mistake. They want you back home. Where you belong."

Riley just shook her head. Her blond hair was dark-ening from the rain, clinging wetly to her cheeks, mak-ing her look impossibly young. Vulnerable. "Why? They're never around, anyway. Dad's campaigning for work and Mom's traveling for work.'' Then she pulled out of Annie's hold and kept walking.

"Where are you going?" Panic raised Annie's voice.

Riley's arms lifted then fell back to her sides. She never looked back.

"She won't go far. Diego's not going anywhere with this weather churning up the way it is."

She jumped, startled at the deep voice. "Where'd you come from?"

Logan smiled faintly and lifted his chin toward the building not ten feet away from where they stood in the middle of the road. "Stopped in at the sheriff's office to say hello to Sam. Couldn't help but notice you and Riley out here." He opened up the black umbrella he held and lifted it over her head.

Annie's gaze followed Riley whose posture—even at the increasing distance—screamed dejection. "I need to go after her."

"Take the umbrella, and get inside soon. Sam said the weather service thinks there's gonna be a bad blow. Storms usually miss Turnabout, but better to be safe."

She hesitated for only a moment. He was there to retrieve Riley, of that she had no doubt. So why was he allowing even a moment of time before doing so?

"Go, Annie," he said quietly. "I'll lock up the shop for you."

She swallowed, turned and went.

It was raining in earnest when Annie reached her house about twenty minutes later. As she let herself inside, her heart was in her throat, nearly choking her. Then she heard the shower running in the single bathroom.

Uncaring of the rainwater dripping from her onto the ceramic-tile floor, she pressed her back against the wall in the hallway and listened to the blessed sound of the bathroom shower. She was shivering. Not just from the chill caused by the rain, but from the past that seemed to loom up in her face no matter how many times she tried to push it behind her.

She slowly slid down until she was sitting on the floor and pressed her wet head back against the wall. Through it she could hear the hiss of the shower even more clearly, as well as the diminishing drum of raindrops on the roof. They grew more sporadic as she listened. Maybe the storm would pass by Turnabout, after all.

The thought was hopeful, but brief, being cut off by a long, crackling rumble of thunder.

From inside the bathroom came the squeak of pipes, the cessation of water, the metallic jangle of shower-curtain rings. By the time the door creaked open several minutes later, Annie was in the kitchen, a clean bath towel slung around her neck, her wet jumper replaced by a sweatshirt and baggy jeans. Riley finally came into the room, her expression wary as Annie pushed a chunky white mug across the breakfast bar toward her.

"What is it?" Riley's voice was suspicious. "Not that weird tea you make out of weeds, I hope."

Annie had quickly found that chamomile tea was *not* a hit with Riley. "Hot chocolate."

"With marshmallows?"

"Is there any other way to drink it?"

Riley crossed to the bar and picked up the mug. She

lifted it carefully. Annie thought she might be smelling it. She took a sip. Followed by a longer one.

"It's good."

"Don't sound so surprised."

"Mom's hot chocolate is awful. No caffeine, no fat, no nothing."

Annie lifted her own mug, her smile growing. Noelle was beautiful and model-thin. There'd been a time or two on Annie's rare visits to their home when she'd heard Will admit to sneaking out for a cholesterol-laden steak and loaded baked potato behind his wife's diet-conscious back.

Riley slipped onto one of the barstools and hunched over the breakfast bar, cradling the mug. "Mom says marshmallows are all sugar."

"When we were kids, your dad wouldn't drink hot chocolate unless the cup was nearly overflowing with marshmallows."

"I'm a lot like him." Riley made the announcement as if it were a sentence being pronounced. "Mom says that all the time. I'm just like *him*." Her lips twisted as she peered into her mug.

"He's a good person," Annie said quietly. "You could do worse than be like Will." Far better that than to be like Annie.

"How come you don't have kids?"

Annie lifted her hot chocolate again and managed to singe her tongue drinking too deeply. It was early afternoon, yet the kitchen was darkening. She flipped on the light. "Some people aren't cut out to be parents," she finally said. "Fortunately, Will and Noelle are."

Riley's expression closed. She turned away from the

counter, bare feet stomping across the tile. A moment later, Annie heard the slam of the bedroom door.

She cursed herself for pushing too far. Sighing, she put her mug on the counter next to Riley's. Neither one of them had finished.

The sliding glass door that led out to the small deck drew her and she moved away from the counter. Outside, the ocean beyond the narrow strip of beach looked gray and forbidding. She opened the door anyway and went out onto the deck. The rain had stopped, but the wind had picked up. Heavy, dark clouds skidded overhead.

The chaise that had seen Annie through more sleepless nights than she cared to count was wet. She pulled the towel from her neck to dry it off, then threw herself down on the seat. The wind tugged at her hair, flinging it around her shoulders. The temperature felt as if it had dropped twenty degrees since that morning. She wished she'd thought to put on socks.

"I told you to get inside."

Her head jerked. Logan had appeared around the side of the small house. He stepped around the elevated frame of her ancient water cistern. When her heart drifted back down from her throat, she chanced speech. "Which explains why you're sneaking around outside my house." Once again, she found herself wishing that he'd do what he'd come to do and go. It would be painful—like the worst kind of bandage being ripped off her skin. But at least it would be quick.

He came toward her, looking even taller from her half-prone position. The wind was doing a number on his hair, too. Blowing through the short, thick strands of dark brown to reveal a few strands of silver. He was as darkly tanned as she remembered. The contrast made his blue eyes seem even brighter. Logan—in the flesh—made her feel as edgy as he ever had.

The sooner he left, the better.

"Riley is inside. You should take her now. You wouldn't want to get stuck on the island if the weather goes even more sour."

"In a hurry to see her go, Annie?" His expression was considering. "Having a teenager around cramping your style?"

She swung her legs off the chaise and rose. "There's no style to cramp. She doesn't belong here with me. She belongs at home with Will and Noelle. Nothing's going to be solved by her remaining here. Everybody, including you, knows that."

"Maybe she just needs a breather. Don't you remember needing a breather when you were her age?"

"When I was her age, I'd already been at Bendle-maier for months. And the last place I wanted to be was at home with George and Lucia."

His lips twisted. He gave her a sidelong look that tightened her stomach. "Liar."

She stiffened. "What?"

He moved, catching her chin in his big palm, tilting it toward him. She went stock-still, her senses going way beyond alert at the close, wind-blown warmth of him.

"You heard me," he challenged softly. "When you were Riley's age, you wanted nothing more than to live at home, to have normal parents who cared more about you than their careers, to go to the same public high school that Will had gone to."

"I never told you that," she said stiffly.

His thumb gently tapped her chin. "You didn't have to tell me everything. It was obvious, Annie. And that night at the boathouse, you said—"

"I said a lot of things." She felt exposed with her face firmly tilted up to his gaze. "And I was drunk," she finished flatly.

"Nearly," he allowed. "On champagne you had no business drinking."

"Well, you were the only one who noticed."

"That pissed you off, too, didn't it?"

She stepped back, deliberately lifting her chin away from his hold. "It was a long time ago and has nothing whatsoever to do with the reason you're here."

"Are you so certain about that?"

Her knees felt weak. She refused to sit, though she wanted to. Badly. "Yes, I'm certain."

The corner of his lips lifted in that saturnine expression of his that visited her too often in her sleep. Ridiculous, really. And maybe it was only because she simply didn't get involved with men—hadn't for more years than she could count on her fingers—that she was beset with memories of this one man in particular.

She'd humiliated herself with him at Will's wedding reception, after all. Her youthfully inflated ego had convinced her that he must surely have had the hots for her, mostly because she hadn't been able to look at him without feeling as if her nerve endings were on fire.

Well, he'd corrected her on that score.

He could have taken advantage of an impetuous and spoiled teenager intent on playing with fire, but he hadn't. So, regardless of the wicked cast of his lips, Annie knew that Logan, like Will, was a straight arrow. Despite his devil-dark looks, he'd probably never even crossed the street against the light.

"Aren't you curious, Annie?"

She snatched at the towel when a gust of wind picked it up off the chaise. She twisted the terrycloth in her hands. "About what? Riley's real reasons for running away from home? It's hard to believe it would just be Bendlemaier. Noelle says that Riley has made a small career out of negotiating things she wants or doesn't want in life."

"That's all you're curious about? Only Riley?" He stepped closer again.

Beyond them, a colorful beach ball hurtled over the sand, followed by a scrap of paper that hung on the wind. For some reason, the sight of them made Annie even more aware of the solitude of her house. Her nearest neighbors were more than a mile away.

She swallowed. "That's all I can afford to be curious about."

"Sounds awfully cautious for the Annie I knew."

Her eyes burned. She blamed it on something in the blowing wind because she didn't cry. Not anymore. "The Annie you knew no longer exists." Her words were barely audible. "She learned her lessons the hard way."

"What lessons?" He jerked his head up before his lips finished forming the question.

An awful buzzing whine had rent the air. Piercing. Loud. Annie nearly jumped out of her skin and covered her ears. "What *is* that?" She had to yell to be heard above the alarm, above the awful thunder that was suddenly crashing overhead, sounding as if mountains were collapsing.

His hand was on her arm, pushing her through the glass door he slid open. "That's the emergency siren. A hangover from the Second World War. Get Riley."

Annie had lived on Turnabout for five years. She hadn't even known there *was* an emergency siren. She ran to the second bedroom and threw the door wide, calling Riley's name.

But the room was empty.

Chapter Four

Annie's heart stopped.

Riley wasn't in her bedroom.

Before she thought about the idiocy of it, she darted into the room, looking under the bed when she knew perfectly well the only things that fitted under there were the shallow plastic storage boxes that contained a lifetime of photographs. She also yanked open the closet door. But all that was inside were her vacuum cleaner and clothing she never wore.

"Riley?" She stumbled around the twin-sized bed to peer out the window that overlooked the front of the house, only to jump back with a cry when a palm branch slammed against it, then screeched along the side of the house as the wind carried it.

Logan was there, arm sliding about her waist, bodily lifting her away from the shuddering windowpane. "Stay away from the glass."

She was beyond listening, twisting away from him, nearly falling over the foot of the bed again as she ran into the hall, calling Riley's name again, barely able to hear her own voice over the wail of the emergency siren.

Darkness seemed to have fallen in the span of minutes, broken by the hideous strobe of lightning that seemed too close and far too dangerous. "She's not in the house." Panic choking her, she headed toward the door, only to find Logan blocking her way. "I have to find her!"

"You don't even have on shoes. I'll go." He reached for the door himself. It blew out of his grasp when he opened it, slamming back against the wall behind it before he caught it again. "Stay here. Inside. She can't be far."

He'd barely disappeared out the door before Annie ran into her bedroom. She shoved her feet into her tennis shoes and followed him.

Her sweatshirt was immediately soaked, her hair whipping around her head, nearly blinding her as she ran around the side of the house. The wind tore Riley's name from her throat, and the siren wailed on and on and on, threatening to madden her.

Where was Riley?

Logan had headed up the path that passed for a road in the front of the house. Annie took the beach behind the house instead. Squinting against the sand that managed to blow despite the deluge of water pounding down on it, she ran past the black, cold fire pit, all the way down to the frothing, roiling edge of water. Peered right and left, staring hard between flashes of light, her heart beating so viciously she felt ill. "Riley!"

But the only thing she saw was an empty ribbon of beach.

Keeping a tenuous grip on common sense, she ran back toward the house. A sob broke out of her throat when her foot caught on a piece of driftwood and she pitched forward in the sand.

She pushed up to her knees, bowing her head against the rain that seemed to blow horizontally, right into her face.

Please, God, let us find Riley safe and sound and I'll take her right back to Will and Noelle. I promise.

Her canvas tennis shoes were full of sand, heavy with water as she unsteadily gained her feet and trudged onward, more carefully this time. Around the side of her small house, sand giving way to gravel, gravel to grass that was drowning in the water that fell too rapidly for the earth to absorb. Her rubber soles slid in the pools of water and she fell again, words coming from her mouth that she had banished from her vocabulary a decade and a half earlier.

She righted herself, shading her eyes with her hands from the storm as she bent against the weight of wind, battling her way to the front of the house, calling Riley's name until her throat ached.

And then she saw Logan in the center of the road.

He was alone, and her stomach dove.

She ran toward him. "I didn't see her on the beach! I don't think she'd have gone toward the water." Riley knew how to swim. Annie had photographs of her as a little girl, wearing a pink polka-dot swimsuit, being coaxed into a swimming pool by Noelle. But surely

Riley would know better than to go near the water now.

Logan caught her arm, pulling her closer to him, seeming to shield her from the brunt of the storm. "I told you to stay inside."

"We have to find her, Logan."

He looked grim. "We will."

Lightning streaked overhead, filling the air with an odd scent. He swore and practically lifted her off her feet as he hauled her farther up the road, away from the palm tree that suddenly burst into flame. She watched, horrified, as it split in half and tumbled to the ground where they'd been standing.

The rain quickly doused the fire.

Annie covered her mouth, staring wildly around them. She didn't have time to be nauseous. Riley was out in this. Alone.

"She can't have made it to town. It'd take too long. Which means, if she's smart, she tried to find some shelter on the way."

Annie shuddered, nodding. "I'm going with you."

He grimaced, but kept hold of her as they headed toward the main road. She was grateful for the support. She'd never felt such wind in her life. Every few steps they managed, it seemed as if the rain switched directions. Blowing straight into their backs one moment. Straight into their faces the next.

Evening was hours off yet, but the clouds were so dense, so heavy, it felt as if night had already fallen. The constant, racking thunder made a mockery of her attempts to call out Riley's name.

"Dammit," Logan cursed, when a river of water

coursed toward them, nearly knocking her off her feet as it washed away the gravel.

"I'm sorry!" She scrambled to maintain her balance. She'd never realized the path was a natural wash before, because it had never rained this much.

He wasn't looking at her. Water streamed off his arm as he lifted it, pointing. "There."

She looked. On the other side of the wash stood an open-sided shack. Sara had told her once that the people who'd built the house where Annie now lived had sold produce at the stand.

"Stay here." Logan's voice was hard. "I'll check it out."

Annie swallowed. In the past decade she'd come to depend only on herself, and this went against every instinct she'd garnered. But she nodded.

He moved away and she realized immediately just how much his tall, broad body *had* shielded her from the storm. The wind plowed into her with such force she felt bruised by it. She slipped and slid her way to the edge of the wash and wedged herself against the boulders that were clustered there.

The water was up to Logan's knees as he crossed against the flood. His progress was slow, but it was steady. Then he made it to the shack.

The wind tore half the roof off and she cried out, watching it head toward him. He lifted his arm across his face, ducking. The wood glanced off him and bounced, end over end, until it slammed into a tree and splintered apart. He didn't stop, though, and disappeared into the shack only to reappear a moment later.

He carried Riley in his arms, running flat out toward Annie, splashing through the torrent.

"She's all right." His deep voice cut through the bellowing storm. "Get back to the house."

Too relieved to argue that she wanted to run her hands over Riley to feel for herself that she was okay, Annie slid away from the boulders and ran. Impossibly, the storm seemed to pick up strength with every step she took. Before she knew it, Logan had grabbed her arm and, still carrying Riley in one arm, nearly carried Annie as well. Beyond the danger of the swelling wash. Past the destroyed palm tree that blocked the lane.

She could hear his harsh breath, and knew hers sounded worse. They nearly skidded across the grass, and Annie darted forward, shoving open the door. It took a death grip to hold it against the wind, as Logan carried Riley inside and set the girl on her feet. Annie surrendered the door to Logan and grabbed her niece in her arms, pulling her close.

"Thank God," she whispered, breathless. "Thank you, God."

"We've gotta find a more secure—" Logan broke off, swearing, when the door blew open again.

Annie let go of Riley long enough to lend her weight against the door. Her wet hands fumbled with the heavy dead bolt that she'd never had cause to use before. It finally slammed home, but still the door rattled and jumped, and she had serious doubts the lock would hold against the punishing wind.

Thinking ahead of her, Logan had grabbed one end of her couch and shoved it up against the door the moment she moved out of the way. "That'll hold it for a while," he muttered. "Only time I remember them setting off the siren was when I was ten years old. Scared the living hell out of me. Everybody went to the school then. Stayed in the basement there."

A thunderous clap shuddered through the house. Windows vibrated. Lord, she didn't want to go back out in that. Fortunately, the road that had become awash didn't head straight toward her house, but they'd still have to cross it to get to town. "We can't make it to the school—" She broke off with a gasp when something crashed against the back side of her house. The glass doors shuddered.

"The bathroom," Logan said abruptly.

She could feel Riley shivering. She rushed the girl back down the short hallway and into the small bathroom, yanking folded towels off the shelf next to the sink as she moved. "Wrap these around you," she told Riley.

"Into the tub."

Annie didn't question Logan. She climbed into the tub. Riley followed, back to Annie, sitting between her legs. Logan flipped the light switch, but the power was definitely gone.

Around them, the house groaned and creaked. The emergency siren ceased as abruptly as it had begun. She contrarily wished it had continued wailing.

"Got candles? Flashlight?"

Annie continued tugging the oversized towels around Riley's shoulders and forced herself to think through her panic. Riley was in front of her, shivering, but safe. That's all that mattered.

"There's a flashlight in the kitchen somewhere," she said shakily. "Maybe the bottom drawer next to the stove. And, um, there are a few candles in my bedroom on the dresser.''

He left.

Riley shivered violently. Annie hugged her arms around her niece. She had a strong desire to screech *what were you thinking* but she battled it down. ''It'll be okay,'' she whispered instead.

The girl sniffled. ''This is supposed to be an island paradise.''

Annie hadn't been seeking paradise when she'd come to Turnabout. Only peace.

She pressed her forehead against the top of Riley's dripping head. Will would never forgive her if something happened to the girl.

She'd never forgive herself.

''Are you hurt anywhere?''

She felt Riley shake her head.

Logan was back in seconds. He handed Annie the flashlight and told Riley to set the candles in the tub in front of her. He also carried a gallon jug of water that Annie had left on the kitchen counter earlier that week. It hadn't fitted in her refrigerator because she was storing Island Botanica products there. He set the jug on the floor then left again.

''He's coming back, isn't he?'' Riley asked a moment later. Her voice was very small.

Annie closed her eyes, wincing with every crack of thunder that shuddered through her little house.. ''Logan won't leave us,'' she promised faintly. Where would he go? Back out into the storm?

He returned quickly, bearing the blanket from Annie's bed as well as several sweaters that he dumped on the ledge beside the tub. Then he muscled the mattress from the guest room's bed into the bathroom.

She wasn't sure what shocked her more. That he'd gone through her drawers to find dry clothing, or that he'd managed to fit a twin mattress into what she'd always considered a frightfully small bathroom.

Logan gestured at Annie and she quickly slid forward, urgency nudging out the shock when he worked his big body into the tub behind her, and pulled the mattress close until it leaned lengthwise against the edge of the tub.

Then he exhaled roughly, and managed to yank his wet shirt over his head. He tossed it beyond the mattress and it fell on the floor with a wet slap.

"Okay, this is getting seriously weird," Riley muttered. She was crunched forward, her legs bent to allow room for the two adults behind her. Her boots thumped against the porcelain. "Don't take anything else off, or I'm outta here."

"Riley, he's as wet as you are."

She huffed, but fell silent.

Logan grabbed the blanket and began working it around Annie's shoulders much the way Annie had wrapped Riley in towels.

"No, wait." Annie tried to hold him off. "You must be cold, too."

Riley huffed again, then yanked one of the towels from her own shoulders and held it back to Annie, who gave it to Logan. "What's with the bed?"

"So we can pull it over our heads if necessary." Logan's voice was matter-of-fact.

"Are you *kidding* me?" Riley's voice rose. "Auntie

Annie, is the house going to blow away or something? This is *Turnabout,* not the freakin' *Wizard of Oz!*''

Annie closed her arms around her niece, enfolding her in the blanket, too. Riley was shaking like a leaf. So was she.

Then Logan closed his arms around her and for a moment, just a brief moment, relief swept through her, calming her own panic just enough that she could sink her claws back into it and keep it under control.

Logan had found Riley.

They were all safe.

"Three men in a boat," Logan muttered. As far as Annie could tell, his breathing was already back to normal, while she still sounded—and felt—as though she'd just run a marathon.

And there they sat while the earth shuddered and the sky seemed to fall down around them. Annie realized she was peering into the hallway, watching the flash of lightning, holding her breath as she felt the steady drum of Logan's heartbeat against her back.

"Turn on the flashlight again," Riley finally begged. "Can we at least turn on a light?"

Annie flipped on the flashlight. Her own panic was starting to weasel out of her hold on it. She couldn't lose it again. There was no time.

No *space!*

She focused on what was physical. Logan, a reassuringly solid presence, his warmth steaming through their soaked clothing. Riley, a soft, trembling weight leaning back against *her,* for comfort.

They'd get through this. It had been a long time since Annie had had *any* storms in her life—this one just happened to be a physical storm, rather than an emotional one. And she'd survived the emotional ones.

More or less.

She tilted her head to look up at Logan, only to find the dark cast of his eyes watching her through the gloomy light.

Annie was suddenly aware of the intimacy of their positions. Of the fact that—beyond the clinging wetness of her sweatshirt and the increasingly damp blanket—his chest was pressed against her back. Hard, wide and feeling damnably perfect.

The kind of chest that could shelter her from a storm.

And had. The thought was tinged with hysteria.

And then, just then, the storm went silent. As if it, too, were holding its breath.

His long fingers skimmed over her cheek and her mouth went dry. She shuddered and the warmth of him against her wasn't merely a barrier against the fear of the storm outside, but something else, entirely.

She felt his chest lift in a deep, long breath.

His fingertips, warm, steady, glided along her jaw. Fleetingly touched the corner of her lips.

She stopped breathing.

Impossible memories of his warm touch, his rough sighs, slipped into her mind. Impossible, because he'd turned her away all those years ago. Impossible, because what they'd shared had lived only in her dreams.

Then he broke the taut moment. "Storm's here," he said, his tone arid. His hand fell away from her face, wrapping instead in the fold of the blanket around Annie's shoulder.

Her breathing kicked in, leaving her feeling dizzy.

Or maybe it was only the effect of the uneven strobe of lightning that filtered into the bathroom from the rest of the house.

Riley made a choked sound. Annie had barely realized it was nervous laughter, when the house heaved a great, wrenching moan.

Logan swore, pushing down on both Annie and Riley as he dragged the mattress over their heads.

Chapter Five

"Oh...my...God."

Annie stared around at what remained of her house. Horror made her dizzy.

They'd stayed cramped in the bathtub, huddled under the suffocating, steamy warmth and protection of the mattress for what had seemed hours. But now, through the gaping hole in her roof, she could see the hint of sunlight trying to break through the clouds, and knew it couldn't have been all that long, after all.

Not until the boisterous racket of the storm ended had Logan pushed aside the mattress, along with an appalling amount of debris and allowed them to unfold their cramped bodies. The worst of the storm seemed to have passed, leaving behind a gentle, misting rainfall.

A rainfall that came right through her house, since there was a good portion of roof missing.

"Geez," Riley muttered, staring at the mess—wallboard, shingles, palm fronds—that had pummeled the mattress and littered the bathroom and hallway. "Serious bummer. Good thing you thought of the mattress," she said. "Otherwise that stuff would've landed on us, huh."

If it weren't for Logan's steadying hand warming the back of her neck, Annie thought she might well pass out. "We don't have tornadoes here," she protested faintly.

"It was probably a downburst or a microburst," he said. His hand left her neck and she blinked, trying to make sense of everything as he grabbed one of the dry sweaters he'd gotten from her room and pushed it into her hands. He looked prepared to dress her in it, as if she were incapable of doing so herself.

She probably was. She went into her room and quickly changed, slipping the limp sweatshirt she wore off and pulling the dry sweater on in its place. It felt heavenly.

But there was nothing to be done about Logan's wet clothes. She had nothing handy that would remotely fit his wide shoulders, and pants were even more out of the question. His shirt still lay in a wet heap on the floor of the bathroom underneath the debris.

But he'd pulled on his leather jacket by the time she rejoined them, and Annie managed to keep her eyes averted from the wedge of hard brown chest that showed above the half-fastened zipper.

"We learned about microbursts in science," Riley was saying. She'd already changed into drier clothes, having escaped the confines of the tub the moment Logan gave the okay. "They can do as much damage

as a tornado, but they don't, you know, twist.'' She
whirled her hand. ''The force just comes straight down
and blows out at the base.'' She shrugged, suddenly
looking uncomfortable at providing them with the science lesson.

Logan nodded as he surveyed the damaged roof.
''We're going to need to cover that roof up before the
rain does even more damage inside.''

''With what? The only wood I have around here is
for burning in the fire pit out on the beach.'' Annie
picked her way through the debris in the short hallway,
fearing what she'd find in the main portion of the
house. She couldn't bring herself even to wonder about
the fields that supplied Island Botanica.

Without their plants, they'd have no products. Without products, they'd have nothing. *She'd* have nothing.
Again.

She deliberately pushed away the dismal thought
and focused on the immediate. The glass door off the
living room looked undamaged. The window in the
kitchen was broken to pieces. Annie's chaise from the
deck poked halfway through it, leaning drunkenly into
the sink below the window. One of her cupboards hung
half off the wall, the door opened to display the broken
glass and dishes inside it.

''Toto, I don't think we're in Kansas anymore,'' Riley said, joining Annie by the breakfast counter. ''All
we need are some flying monkeys and the wicked
witch and it'd be like we're living inside the *Wizard
of Oz* movie. How are you going to get all this fixed
again?''

''I always hated those flying-monkey things,'' Annie murmured instead of answering something she had

no answer for. "They gave me nightmares." The two half-full mugs of chocolate still sat on the counter, twin sentries oblivious to the tempest that had occurred around them. The marshmallows had melted into the liquid.

She went around the counter, picked up the mugs and reaching through the legs of the chaise, dumped the cold cocoa down the sink. When she turned away, Logan was watching her, his expression strangely gentle as he set the gallon jug of water that he'd rescued on the countertop. "Try to make that last," he suggested. "I'm going to town to see if I can find something to cover the holes in the roof."

Annie nodded and moved around the counter to look through the unscathed glass door. If she tried to speak, she feared she would burst into tears. She hadn't cried in years and she had no intention of starting up again.

"Want to come with me?"

She turned around, only to realize that Logan had offered the invitation to Riley.

"Why? So you can drag me off the island?"

He just looked at the teen and finally she made a face and shrugged. "Whatever."

Logan moved the couch away from the front door, positioning it back where it belonged. It had done the job, at least, of keeping the door from flying open. He stopped to pick up a potted fern that had tipped over, spilling soil onto the tile.

"We won't be long. Don't try to pick up anything that's not stable." As if his words were prophetic, the loose cabinet in the kitchen gave a squeal of splitting wood and plunged to the floor, bouncing off the counter along the way.

Shattered glassware and dishes flew.

Annie choked back a shocked yelp and turned her gaze from the sight.

Riley was the first to break the thick silence. "Well that sucks. Hope that wasn't the family china or something."

Annie shook her head. "I think I'll go with you, too," she said. "There may be houses hit worse than mine. People who might need help."

The thought was somber and the three of them left the house in silence. Outside, it was still drizzling, and Annie ran back inside long enough to grab her umbrella from its hook in the coat closet as well as a bright yellow slicker. She told Riley to put on the slicker, then opened the umbrella and Logan held it over all three of them.

The water that had flooded the narrow road had already narrowed to a trickle. The sun was beginning to set, bathing the thick ribbons of clouds and everything below them with an otherworldly cast of red and orange.

Annie's feet dragged as she stepped over the felled palm tree. The vivid sky seemed all the more remarkable because of the rainbow that glittered, looking close enough to touch.

Rainbows were supposed to be a sign of hope, weren't they? But as she watched, the wondrous arch faded, leaving only the sunset behind.

Logan stopped, too. "Turnabout always did have unbelievable sunsets. The best view was from the Castillo House, though, at the point of the island. Old place probably doesn't even exist anymore."

"Yes, it does." Annie had a particular interest in

the abandoned Mission-style house, but she was more concerned with Riley, who'd walked on ahead of them, only to stop and wait near the very boulders that had kept Annie from blowing away earlier. She put thoughts of rainbows—and hope—right out of her mind as reaction set in, making her shake at the awful "what ifs."

"She thinks she's too cool to walk underneath the umbrella," he said.

"I should have marched her right back to Will and Noelle," she said. "The day she showed up. Instead of *calling* my brother, I should have taken her back myself."

"She's okay, Annie. She's not hurt. She's probably feeling pretty foolish for leaving the house, too."

"She's okay only because you were there and knew what to do. You found her. Brought her back to the house. It never would have occurred to me to use a bathtub and a mattress for protection."

"You'd have found her if I hadn't. You'd have thought of something."

She was beyond listening, though, as she sloshed through the water and hurried up the gravel. "Riley should never be in danger. Ever. She's just a girl, a baby. Completely innocent and undeserving of—"

"Hey." He closed his hand around her shoulder and halted her. "No kid deserves to be in danger. But this was a storm. A freakish one. You didn't wiggle your pretty nose and summon it. And it's not like you can protect your niece from *life*."

Why not? Annie barely kept from crying out the words as they heard a vehicle and the distinctive crunch of tires on gravel. In seconds, the sheriff's truck appeared and Sam Vega stuck his head out the window. "Yo, Annie. Everybody okay at your place?"

Avoiding Logan's eyes, Annie jogged over to the olive-drab vehicle. "We're not hurt," she assured shakily. "What about in town?"

Sam looked grim. "We've got a dozen or so injuries, so far, the least of which is Janie. She was trying to save some of her special glass and ended up breaking her wrist, instead. I'll know more once I've made it across the isle to check on everybody. A lot of windows broke in the winds, but most of the buildings are okay. Your shop'll need some boarding up. Got a report that Diego's dock is history, though. I haven't been by your fields yet."

"The dock?" Dismay settled like a stone inside her. Her fields overlooked the dock. "What about Diego's boats?" She struggled to keep her voice steady.

"Out of commission for a while," Sam said. His gaze went past her to Logan. "If somebody *has* to get on or off the island, it'll be by Coast Guard."

She could feel the edges of her sanity unraveling. "What about a plane? A charter? When Dr. Trahern and his wife took April Fielding off for surgery last year, they did it in a plane that landed on the main road." Her brother had connections and plenty of money. He could arrange a plane or a helicopter for Riley's sake. Cell phones didn't work out on the island, and the phone lines were undoubtedly down along with the electricity, but surely if the sheriff could reach the Coast Guard, they could manage a way to contact her brother.

"And that plane tore the hell out of the road, which wasn't in great shape to begin with. Even a chopper would have to be an emergency, Annie. The coastline is socked in from Mexico on up. We'll be lucky if this—'' Sam's gesture encompassed the destruction that had already occurred ''—is all we have to contend with. Before we lost communications, the weather service was warning that several storm systems were on a collision course with each other. The weather's bad here. It's worse on the mainland. They've got straight winds that are tearing the hell out of San Diego.''

And Sara was in San Diego. Annie pressed her hand to her mouth, struggling for composure.

''She wants to get Riley home to her parents,'' Logan said.

Sam shook his head. ''Riley is physically unharmed. On a scale of priorities for getting to the mainland, that means she's not going to be at the top. I'm sorry, Annie, but that's just the way it is. Hugo can do a lot with those who are injured, but his clinic is small and underequipped. Anybody needing more serious medical attention will be the first to go. My suggestion to you is to try to board up the windows at your shop—''

''And her roof at home,'' Logan added.

''—whatever needs doing,'' Sam's gaze took in Logan also, ''and hunker down. At best, we've got a few days of cleanup. At worst...'' He shook his head, obviously not wanting to elaborate. ''So, if you guys are okay, I've gotta head on. I'll come back when I can and we'll get that palm dragged off the road.''

Annie nodded and stepped away from the truck. She heard Logan offer his assistance should Sam need it, then he, too, stepped back. Sam reversed his truck up the gravel, passing by Riley who'd perched herself on the boulders to wait, and headed off into the shadows.

The light from the truck's headlights bounced over the scrubby bushes lining the hillside, seeming to reflect back on the truck because of the wall of mist shrouding the landscape.

Annie swept back her damp hair and headed toward Riley. "I need to see how bad the fields are." She didn't wait to see if Logan followed.

Of course, he did.

Riley slid off the boulder when they reached her. She said nothing, but apparently it was dark enough to quell her worry over appearing cool, for she fell into step alongside Annie underneath the protection of the umbrella that Logan still held.

The fields were in the opposite direction to the town and it was dark by the time they got there. With no moonlight to guide them, it was impossible to see what sort of damage they'd sustained. She closed her eyes against what she couldn't see and battled back fear of the worst.

Logan's hand touched her shoulder. "We'll come back when it's light."

Annie's eyes burned. She moved. His hand fell away.

They turned toward town, walking down the center of the roughly paved road that would lead them straight into the heart of Turnabout. When they reached it, people were walking up and down in front of the storefronts, circles of illumination from their flashlights bobbing along as they checked businesses and property.

She wished again that she'd thought to bring the flashlight, but she'd forgotten it in the tub when Logan had pushed back the mattress.

"What are they doing over there?" Riley pointed toward the community center across the street from them. Affectionately dubbed the "biggest building on Turnabout" by the residents even though it really was no such thing, the center had its doors opened wide. A fire burned in the domed iron fireplace outside the building and in the light from that, Annie recognized several people carrying boxes of every size through the doors.

"Taking supplies to a central point," Logan said.

"Riley, why don't you go on over there," Annie suggested. "The community center has a generator of its own. I don't imagine it will take long for someone to get it going. And there's no point in you freezing out here while I check the shop."

Riley hesitated. But a group of teenagers huddled around the heat of the fire, and after a moment, she headed toward them.

Annie watched long enough to see her niece approach the group, then, just as easily get swallowed into it. Relieved, she turned away, glancing at Logan as they set off for her shop near the other end of the string of businesses. "I'm glad she's not shy. It's debilitating."

"You were never shy a day in your life." Logan caught her arm when her shoe caught on a bump in the dark sidewalk.

"Yes, I was. Painfully." She hurried her step, mostly to get away from Logan's hand since her imagination was telling her that her arm was tingling beneath her thick sweater.

"You were born to be the life of the party."

She crossed her arms, surreptitiously rubbing that

spot on her elbow. Apparently, her imagination was
really in fine form. "I learned to *act* the life of the
party," she corrected wearily. "It was easier to do that
than let anyone see what I was really like."

"And it got George and Lucia's attention more effectively?"

Annie lifted her shoulder, neither agreeing nor dis-
agreeing. She didn't like talking about her parents.
She'd been an enormous disappointment to them. She
cast a look his way, wanting to get the subject off
herself. She'd been foolish for even touching on her
past. "What were you like as a teenager?"

"When I wasn't running down Maisy's trees at the
inn, you mean? I'd have thought Sara would have
filled you in chapter and verse."

"Like we had nothing more interesting to talk about
than you?"

"I'm wounded." He pressed his hand to his chest.
But she'd caught the gleam of his teeth and heard the
smile in his voice.

It charmed her.

And she didn't want to be charmed. Particularly by
a man who would be leaving Turnabout as quickly as
possible. "You don't have to come with me to the
shop. I'm capable of screwing in some planks of plywood over my windows if need be."

"And where are you going to get the sheets of
wood?"

"I have some in my workroom, if you must know.
And even if I didn't, I'm sure someone else would
have some. Turns help each other out when it's called
for."

"You weren't born on Turnabout. Therefore, you're

not officially a Turn,'' he said smoothly. ''You might consider yourself an islander now, but that doesn't change facts and make you a Turn.''

''No, but your sister is a Turn, and she's my business partner. Courtesies get extended to me as a result.''

He snorted softly. ''Honey, you're dreaming if you think the die-hards of this place will ever truly accept you. They have too much respect for the Turnabout curse that says Turns and outsiders don't mix. That curse has been around a helluva lot longer than you have.''

''Spoken with all the sureness of being a Turn yourself,'' Annie scoffed, even though she secretly feared there was a grain of truth in his words. Though she felt a part of the community, there still remained a lingering sense that she was not entirely accepted. Trusted.

''I wasn't born on Turnabout,'' Logan said. ''I'm no more a Turn than you are.''

Her toe caught another buckle in the sidewalk right in front of the broken plate-glass window of her shop. She barely kept herself from pitching forward onto her nose, and was grateful when she didn't. She already felt as if she'd been hit by a truck. ''But Dr. Hugo is a Turn, and so is your sister.''

''So?''

''Well, where were you born, then?''

''Oregon.''

She didn't remember Sara ever mentioning Oregon. ''Your family must have lived there before Sara was born, I guess.''

''My parents were separated for a while. They reunited after I was born," he said flatly. "Now, do you want to show me where this plywood of yours is, or should I head through the shop window like a bull and find it myself?"

Feeling well and truly put in her place by his tone, Annie unlocked the door. Though Logan had been right; they could just as easily have walked in through the window that no longer existed. Despite the darkness, she found her way across the retail front, and was relieved that the racks and cases seemed to be where they belonged.

In the workroom, she took a candle from the stock shelves and felt through the jumble atop the desk for one of the lighters that Sara was forever stealing from her father. Annie had always wondered why Sara bothered, considering that Hugo never did use his lighters for his cigars. But for now, she was glad of it when she found one and used it to light the candle.

She set it on the desk then lit a few more, until there was a soft, warm glow inside the workroom. She pointed to the pallets in the farthest corner of the room, beyond the oven they often used to help dry herbs.

"Plywood," she said. "Sara and I had it shipped here a few months ago. We're planning to build more shelves back here for the stock, but we haven't gotten to it, yet."

He moved toward the pallets, ducking to keep from knocking his head into the bundles hanging by string from the frame that hung suspended from the high ceiling. "Handy for us," he said.

Annie found the toolbox and brought it out to the front while Logan carried a sheet of wood. She winced anew at the crunch of glass beneath their shoes. "What a mess. And," she lifted a forestalling hand, "I know. It could be a whole lot worse. I have no reason to complain." Of course, she hadn't seen her fields, yet, either.

"I didn't say anything."

"You didn't have to." She held the door so he could carry the wood outside, then knelt down to open up the toolbox. "I can hear the judgment in your voice." She pulled out her cordless drill and handed it to him, then poked through the contents of the box until she found the jar of screws. She also found a tiny metal flashlight and flipped it on, but the batteries were dead. She tossed it back into the toolbox.

His shoulder held the plywood against the building as he took the jar and flipped off the lid. "Believe me, I'm in no position to judge anyone." Finding a few screws that satisfied him, he set the jar on the ground, then lifted the wood into place. In seconds, he'd secured it. Then he went back inside for another sheet, came out, and repeated the process. Soon, there were three large sheets of wood covering the gaping hole.

"Might as well wait until it's light to clean up the glass inside," he said as she came out with a push broom to clean off the sidewalk as best she could. He reached for it, but she didn't let go.

"I'm perfectly capable of sweeping up the mess."

"And apparently, you're capable of building your own stock shelves," he said, and deftly slipped the broom handle from her grasp. "I noticed you didn't say that you and Sara planned to have shelves *built,* but that you planned to *build* them." He shook his head a little. "Who would've thought?"

Annie crossed her arms and leaned back against the

covered window, watching him work. She enjoyed it a little more than was comfortable.

Logan Drake had always been impossibly good-looking. Now, in dark jeans and a leather jacket, with his hair messy, his jaw bristled, and his hands capably dealing with wood and power tools, he was lethal. "You're a chauvinist," she observed faintly.

His laugh was short. "If that means I think men have a duty to protect women, then I s'pose I am."

She looked away from the way his jacket gaped against his chest. "But women aren't capable of protecting men?"

"Didn't say that."

"Or that men can't protect men? Or women protect women? And I'm not talking about personal relationships, here."

He paused, lifting his head to watch her through the darkness. "Neither am I. And believe me, Annie, there are men who'll protect men at *all* costs."

Disquiet sneaked through her, displacing her unsettling preoccupation with his physical appeal. There was something decidedly dark in his tone. "Speaking from experience?"

She thought he wouldn't answer. He began pushing the broom again. Then finally his motions ceased. Just for a moment. He looked at her, and she felt as if that look seeped into her very pores, filling her right down to her toes with a strange sense of sorrow.

"Yes," he said quietly. "I speak from experience."

Chapter Six

"Heard you were back, Logan."

"Good to see you back, Logan."

"Finally came home, eh, Logan?"

How many times had Logan heard variations of that particular comment? And how many times had he shaken his head and assured the greeter that he was only visiting?

Too damned many.

It was well after midnight and the community center—a hive of activity for hours—was now nearly silent. A dozen lanterns had been placed around the large interior to help save the load on the generator that would have to last for who knew how many days. Now, the lanterns were dimmed as low as they could go without being extinguished, and in the faint glow they emitted, Logan looked around.

Victims of the storm were settled in on cots, borrowed sleeping bags and donated bedrolls. There were no crying babies at the moment and no more gales of laughter that more often than not had verged on the edge of hysteria.

Outside the still-open community center doors, the fireplace was dark. Despite the protective dome, the flame hadn't been able to sustain itself when the rain went beyond mist to drops, to deluge. He could still hear the rain, but now there was no damaging wind, no lightning strikes.

At least he'd managed to get the sheet plastic down in time over the holes in Annie's roof, though it'd been close. He'd managed only because Maisy had sent her handyman, Leo Vega, along in a golf cart to help him soon after he'd finished up with the boards over Island Botanica's window.

While Annie and Riley stayed in town and continued helping out where they could, Logan, Leo and a half dozen other men from around town had made the rounds, including Annie's place. They'd covered windows and roofs, using up even Annie's leftover plywood on the worst, but some places had been damaged beyond repair.

And despite the work that had required all of their energy, there had still been plenty of talking going on.

Some things about Turnabout didn't change at all. The grapevine was one of them. Without trying—and he had definitely *not* been trying—he'd heard about Dante Vega being up for parole again, about Diego's latest bass-fishing trip and about the looker who'd arrived barely a week ago to stay at Maisy's Place who seemed extraordinarily curious about the people and places on the dinky island.

And once they'd gotten on the subject of females, the talk really took off. From Darla Towers who'd just gotten a divorce because she was bedding any guy who'd smile her way, to Annie Hess who'd freeze out any guy stupid enough to look her way.

With a little pressure, Logan learned from Leo that he'd been working on getting Annie to go out with him for more than a year, with no success.

Even though he knew Leo—several years younger than his brother, Sam—from way back, Logan had wanted to nudge the guy off the roof they'd been covering. He'd satisfied himself with the egging comments Leo had gotten from some of the other guys that maybe Annie Hess's refusals of Leo had more to do with her good taste than with a lack of passion.

Logan rubbed his hand down his face, brushing away the thoughts. It seemed a helluva lot longer than twenty-four hours since he'd been in Will Hess's office, thinking he'd been given a convenient opportunity to make up for a long-ago sin by retrieving Will's runaway daughter.

Annie sat down beside him with a rustle of her baggy denim jeans. She let out a long sigh, then tilted her head to look at him.

The wetter it had gotten outside, and the drier inside, the wavier her hair had become. Now, in the lantern glow, it looked as shining as moonlight, as soft as spiraled cotton.

Little more than twenty-four hours, he thought, and he had sinning on his mind all over again.

"You okay?" Her voice was barely a whisper.

He was a damned fool, is what he was. "Yeah."

She stretched out her legs, then a moment later drew them back up. Nervous energy radiated from her, and she betrayed it further with the hand she brushed through her hair, causing the curls to spring even more fully to life.

Her hair always had been incredible. He still remembered the way it had felt winding around his fingers when he'd sunk his hands into it. As if it were yesterday instead of more than a dozen years ago.

He quietly thumped his head against the wall behind him.

"I can't believe the storm nearly leveled the Seaspray Inn." Her soft voice pulled at him. "It's a miracle there weren't more injuries. I heard the man who had a heart attack during the storm is doing well, though, at your dad's clinic. Dr. Hugo's been working nonstop."

"A real saint," Logan drawled.

Her gaze glided over him, snagging when it met his. She moistened her lips, and pushed her hand through her hair again, looking away.

"Maisy had some vacancies," Logan told her. He knew he was keeping the conversation going only because he wanted her to look at him again, so he could see the soft, pink sheen of her lips. "The guests displaced from the Seaspray have filled her cottages to the top. Some of the residents took in people, too."

"I heard. I don't know why, but I always have to remind myself that you and Sara are related to Maisy Fielding."

"By marriage." He held a lot more fondness for

Maisy than he did for his own father, that was for damned sure.

She'd closed her arms around her up-drawn knees and she rested her cheek on top of them. Her hair drifted over her shoulders. "She and your father are an item, you know. They have been for some time now."

"I've heard." It had been yet another topic for gossip during that evening.

"What do you think about it?" If possible, her voice was even softer.

"I thought she had better taste."

"What's the problem between you and your dad, anyway?"

He looked at her.

"Well, you pretty much know what the problem was between me and *my* parents." She was matter-of-fact. "I was a total screwup where they were concerned."

"Sitting on the floor in the big building in the middle of the night must make you feel chatty."

Her lips twitched. She turned her head, looking around. "The cots and bedrolls are all used up."

"I saw Riley with some other teenagers watching a few toddlers."

"Yes. She asked if she could stay here, keep helping with the children tomorrow while the parents continue the cleanup. She seemed genuinely interested in helping. I figured it was okay."

He frowned, wondering if it was his imagination, or if Annie really thought she needed to justify her decision. "She seems like a good kid." Despite worrying her entire family and the devil-take-you attitude. The few kids he'd ever had cause to have dealings with had definitely *not* been of the "good" variety. And having Riley in the middle of several dozen Turns was about as safe a place as she could be.

"She *is* good. And maybe if she feels useful, she won't try anything foolish again." She fell silent for a long moment, then abruptly rolled to her feet. "Well, I'm out of here." She pushed back her hair again. Lifted her lips in a bad imitation of a smile and started to leave.

He rose, grimacing at the stiffness in his joints from sitting on the floor. He caught up with her near the still-opened doors, stopping her short with a hand on her arm.

Her wary gaze skipped over him, taking in the room beyond them. "Is there s-something you need?"

"A bed."

"Well, all the cots are used, I think, but maybe there's a—"

"Spare bed at your place," he interrupted her. "If Riley's here tonight that means you've got a spare."

Her curls shimmered in the pale-gold light as she shook her head. "No. Absolutely not. I appreciate everything you've done today, but...*no*."

He saw several heads rise up from sleeping bags and cots to look their way. He waited long enough for them to settle back down before he spoke again, keeping his voice low. "There's no floor space left to sleep here, and your house is in better shape than some." He had no desire to sleep on the floor in the community center, though he'd slept in worse places. But tonight, he was determined, and it had a lot more to do with Annie than with finding a softer place to rest his old bones.

"It's the least you can do after today, don't you think?"

"Sleep at Sara's place."

"According to the manly gossip-session I was blessed to hear, Sara doesn't own a bed. She sleeps in a hammock. And how the hell Leo Vega knows that is something we'll have to have a talk about later."

"No."

"You're going to turn away an old friend, Annie? The brother of your best friend?"

She gave a little start, and took a step back. "We're not friends, we're hardly acquaintances. And if anybody else said that, they'd sound like they were whining."

He almost laughed at that. They both knew he wasn't whining. And they both knew he wouldn't be dissuaded. Lastly, he wasn't going to get into an argument about "what" they were.

Annie Hess was not going home alone tonight. They had unfinished business, and he wanted that rectified before he took Riley back where she belonged. "I'm coming with you, so pocket the outrage for now—unless you want to stand here and keep whispering as if we're ten-year-olds cheating during a math test. I want a bed. You've got one." And he'd be smarter this time around. Which was maybe why he *was* so determined. To prove he could be stronger, smarter, than he had been before.

She jerked her arm out of his hold and spun on her heel. Her tennis shoes squeaked loudly against the hard floor as she hurried through the doorway, which drew another round of lifted heads and curious eyes.

She was standing by the cold fireplace when he followed. He pushed the doors nearly closed, then held up a small key ring. "Leo's golf cart." He started toward the vehicle.

"Did he lend the keys to you, or did you browbeat him into it?" She hurried after him, her voice an angry whisper above the soft scuff of their shoes on the wet, grass-sprigged gravel.

"Does it matter?" He slid into the cart and turned the key. The motor turned over with a faint whine. "Get in. You're getting soaked again from the rain." He felt around on the dark panel in front of him for some sort of light, but apparently the old cart didn't come equipped with one.

"I suppose this is another example of how you protect women?"

"It's a fact that I intend to sleep on a reasonably comfortable, reasonably dry mattress tonight," he said.

She finally huffed, then moved around to the driver's side. "Move over," she said flatly. "I don't want you driving off a cliff, and you won't be able to see the road at all considering how dark it is."

"I doubt the road has changed in the past fifty years," Logan countered, but he moved to the passenger seat. She climbed in the driver's seat, setting the cart into motion with a jerk. Then she twisted the wheel, veering around a bicycle lying on the gravel.

"When's the last time *you* drove?"

"Shut up."

His lips twitched with a jolt of amusement. That was more like the Annie he knew. She'd been a firebrand. Set on having her way, no matter what obstacles she might encounter. Including him.

His comment notwithstanding, however, she did

drive capably, unerringly, despite the bumps and pot-
holes, the mud puddles and storm debris. And she
didn't say a word to him. It was as if she were pretending he wasn't beside her, their thighs and shoulders brushing whenever she hit a bump in the road.

Shortly after she turned down the gravel lane toward
her little beach house, she veered around the palm tree
blocking it, took a short cut to her front door via the
patch of waterlogged lawn, and stopped so abruptly he
figured she lost a foot of turf under the wheels because
of it. She slipped from behind the wheel. He heard,
more than saw her disappear inside the house. The
latch of the closing door was barely audible above the
beat of rain, and he wished that she'd just slammed
the door instead.

The Annie of old would have done that.

This Annie, the one who lived the quiet existence
he'd heard about again and again that evening, was
something—some*one*—he didn't have a handle on yet.

Logan ran his hand down his face. Slicked back his
wet hair. Sighed.

Then he followed her inside.

She'd already lit a few candles—probably the same
ones he'd taken from her dresser earlier that day—and
they sat on the breakfast bar, casting a small glow that
danced off the modest furniture to birth a dozen shadows. He headed down the hall, stopping short when
she stepped out of the bathroom, the flashlight in her
hand. She turned it on and aimed it at his face.

"How much did Will pay you to come get Riley?
Whatever it is, I'll pay you double. If you'll just go
away. As soon as the ferry is running again, I'll make
sure she gets home myself."

"Thought you didn't want to force Riley into going where she didn't want to go." Will had told him that.

"Yes, well, obviously I was wrong. She'll be safer at home. So…how much?"

He narrowed his eyes against the glare of light. "I didn't take anything from Will. My time is not for sale." Which wasn't strictly accurate. "And even if it was, you couldn't afford it." Which was definitely accurate.

She made a scoffing sound, and he grabbed her hand, intending to redirect the beam of light away from his eyes.

But he felt her hand shake.

He gentled his movement, sliding his fingers around hers, slipping away the flashlight with his other hand and turning the beam toward the floor.

"Are you cold?" It was dry inside the house, and chilly, but not nearly as bad as it was outside. "Too bad you don't have a fireplace."

"I'm not cold."

He tightened his hand around hers. "You're shivering."

"Fine, then. I'm cold." Her tone was short. She tugged her hand away from his, and turning sideways slid past him toward the smaller of the two bedrooms.

He heard a thump, a muffled oath, the squeak of a drawer. He directed the flashlight through the doorway to see her dump something bulky on the box spring. A quilt, he guessed.

"You'll need to get the top mattress out of the bathroom," she said, and moved past him again. "Since I have no idea how you fitted it in there in the first place.

And I doubt it'll be very comfortable anyway. The side that was up during the storm is filthy."

She was all business.

Except that she'd been shivering. Trembling.

And her hand had not been cold.

"I'll manage," he murmured. She'd headed back to the candlelit kitchen. He watched her crouch down on the floor next to the fallen cupboard and ruined dishes. She didn't go for a broom, didn't reach out to rescue any salvageable items. Just sat there, hunkered down on her heels, strands of her hair gleaming in the dim candle glow, her arms wrapped around herself.

Not to hold the cold at bay, but to hold in the trembling?

"These dishes were one of the first things I bought when I was on my own," she said after a moment, obviously aware that he was watching her. "My apartment was a tiny studio. No bedrooms. I didn't have furniture; just two folding chairs, a card table. An air mattress. One of those blow-up things that people use for camping. I'd stick it in the closet during the day. It wasn't much, but it was a home of my own creating. And I bought this set of dishes." She shook her head a little. "Silly, isn't it? Riley hoped they weren't the family china."

"These mattered to you more."

"Yes." Her voice was painfully soft. "Goodness knows, my mother would never have trusted me with her china."

"Your mother was a bitch."

He heard her suck in a breath. Slowly let it out. Then she pushed to her feet, stepping away from the mess in the kitchen. She stopped in front of him, keeping a good foot of distance between them. "If Will isn't paying you to retrieve Riley, then why are you doing it, Logan? You don't strike me as a man who owes anyone favors. So why are you really here?"

"You have to ask?" Yeah, Cole had asked him to take this on, but Logan could have refused to come to Turnabout if he'd wanted to.

He hadn't.

He still didn't know why. Curiosity? Stupidity? Or more likely that he had never fully gotten Annie out of his head.

She crossed her arms. Uncrossed them. "Apparently, I do have to ask." She crossed them yet again. "Is it your family? Sara's doing fine, you know. She misses you, I think, but she's in a good place in her life. And Dr. Hugo—"

"I'm not here because of them."

"Then why? Why get involved in another Hess mess?" She hesitated for a moment, looking pained. "I may have thrown myself at you *years* ago, but I have no desire to repeat that."

"Really?" He could practically sense the fine hair on her arms standing at attention because of the tension passing between them. She'd been too young all those years ago. But that couldn't be said now. And there was no pretending the chemistry wasn't alive and well between them.

"I don't go around asking for second helpings of humiliation," she said flatly. "One was more than enough."

His laugh was short on humor. "Humiliation? You? Come on, Annie, I'm the one who couldn't—"

"Stop!" She lifted her hand.

Exactly, he thought grimly. He hadn't stopped. And he damned well should have.

But she was talking again, looking vaguely desperate and entirely exhausted. "Let's just forget about it, okay? It was a long time ago. I'd just as soon forget it ever happened."

"Believe me, darlin', so would I. Unfortunately, I haven't quite mastered it." The memory of that night had dogged him ever since.

"Good grief. It was a long time ago, Logan. I was seventeen years old and I threw myself at you shamelessly. But you're the original good guy. You weren't interested. You'd never do anything unsavory." She shook her head, her lips turning down at the corners. "If you weren't, we'd have been lovers sixteen years ago." She thrust back her hair and turned away from him. She picked up a candle and headed down the hall.

He stood there in her quiet kitchen, listening to the faint sounds of her moving around in her bedroom, the soft whoosh of the ocean beyond her back door.

She didn't remember.

The night that had haunted him for sixteen long years simply didn't exist for her.

Chapter Seven

Her heart thudded. Her skin felt too tight. For hours—days—she'd wanted to taste his kiss. To feel his body against hers. To touch him. He was different than anyone else. Especially Drago. And now was her chance.

She pushed herself up on her elbow and leaned over his prone body. There. She slid her fingers through his thick hair, carefully drawing it off his forehead. "Kiss me," she whispered.

He didn't reply.

Then she would kiss him. She leaned over him, hesitating for a breathless moment as her breasts pressed against his chest. Then she slid upward, nearly crying in delight at the feel of his chest hair—crisp yet soft— against her tight nipples. Feeling dizzy, she quickly pressed her mouth to his.

His lips were soft. Pliable. She felt his chest lift in a deep breath. She curved her body more closely against his. Nothing had ever felt as good, as strong, as steady as he did. She kissed him, aching for him to lift his hands, to hold her. Tell her that he felt the same, that he cared.

But he stubbornly remained silent.

She drew her leg up his, catching her breath at the sensation. Roughened by hair, and oh, so very warm. Her head swam. Before she backed out, she quickly shifted, slipping over him.

Oh. She weakly dropped her head forward, resting against his chest. Knowing what to expect in theory was a whole lot different in reality.

A whole lot better.

He made a low sound and caught her hips in his hands, pressing up against her. Yes. He was just as she'd imagined. Better. Hard where she was soft. Strong where she was not.

Before she could chicken out, she slid her hand down his side, his hip, where his skin felt impossibly smooth. She reveled in the varied textures of his body for a breathless eon. Then she shifted, reached between their bodies. Found him.

He felt hot. Hard.

For her.

She exhaled, truly shaken with want. For the first time in her life. "Now, Logan. Now, please."

He turned her, suddenly. Colors spun in her head. And then he was over her, his mouth on hers, his hands fisting in her hair—

Annie opened her eyes with a start, sitting bolt upright in the middle of her bed.

Her fingers dug into the mattress beneath her. She was on Turnabout. In her own room. In her own house that smelled—impossibly—of coffee.

She was alone.

She exhaled shakily and slowly relaxed her grip. Her eyes felt gritty and dry from too little sleep. Weak sunlight filtered through the unadorned window beside her bed, and she automatically reached over to turn on the small lamp sitting on the bedside table.

The bulb remained dark.

The electricity was still out.

She fell back against the pillows, bending her arm over her eyes. Could half a night of dreams as tangled as the bedding that twisted about her legs cause the imagined smell of coffee?

Somehow, she doubted it.

Which meant that Logan was out there finding some creative way of brewing coffee that smelled heavenly. She usually preferred the herbal teas she and Sara produced, but right now, her nerves were crying for a solid jolt of caffeine.

She groaned softly and turned her face into her pillow. If only the previous day had been as unreal as the dream. She'd long ago accepted that the dream was a defense against a reality that so shamed her she couldn't bring herself to recall it. But this time, the dream had been particularly...lifelike.

It's just because you knew that Logan was sleeping on the other side of the wall behind your bed. Just because you were exhausted after lying awake most of the night.

Right. All the excuses in the world couldn't make her forget that, even now, her body hummed.

She was torn between wanting to stay in bed with her head buried like an ostrich in the sand and a need to put herself as far away from the bed and dreams of Logan as possible. She knew from experience that the ostrich approach would accomplish nothing. And the dreams were nothing more than a defense.

The day before *had* happened. The week before *had* happened. The mistakes of her past *had* come back to haunt her.

So she pushed aside the sunny yellow blanket that she'd retrieved from the bathroom tub-shelter when she'd left Logan standing in her living room the night before. She untwisted the white sheet from her legs and forced herself out of the bed.

Unfortunately, every movement she made awakened a host of aches from head to toe. And alerted her to the fact that it was freezing.

She replaced her flannel pajamas with thick sweatpants and sweatshirt. Then added another sweatshirt over the first. She pushed her feet into rubber-soled socks and padded out of her room, stopping briefly in the plastic-roofed bathroom. One glimpse of herself in the mirror over the sink was enough to shock her back to her ostrich position in her bed, but she resisted the urge.

She wrangled her hair into a clip at the back of her head, and warily tried the faucet. Water spat from it, then eventually ran in a thin, clear trickle.

Hallelujah. She'd never felt more thankful for her antiquated water cistern.

Still, she didn't waste a drop as she quickly brushed her teeth and washed her face. Feeling somewhat more alert, she went in search of the fragrant coffee with a silent, fervent assurance to herself that she did *not* care if Logan thought she looked as bad as she knew she did.

That assurance fizzled the moment his shocking-blue gaze looked at her over the mug he had lifted to his mouth. He lowered the mug, revealing the amused tilt of his lips. ''Morning, sleeping beauty.''

She briefly considered baring her teeth. Why was it that men like Logan actually improved—a feat in itself—under circumstances like these? He hadn't shaved, his clothes looked as if he'd slept in them—which he probably had. And he still looked like fantasy-fodder.

Or dream-dweller.

She focused on the green metal camp stove sitting on top of the real stove. A blackened coffee pot sat on one burner, and a large saucepan on the other. The cupboard and mess of broken dishes had been cleared away.

Obviously Logan's doing.

She walked past him and looked into the pan on the camp stove. It contained water that was just coming to a boil. ''You've been to town?'' Obviously he had, since she didn't *own* a camp stove.

She should have awakened earlier. Gone to town herself. Checked on Riley.

Checked on a way to get Riley home as quickly as possible.

''Yeah. I went by your fields, too. I'm no master gardener, but I didn't see much damage that a few days of sun won't cure. The town's a mess, though. Looks even worse in the daylight.''

Her knees felt weak. "Thanks for checking the fields. Did you see Riley when you were in town?"

"Yeah. Maisy's put her and some other kids to work, keeping April and some of her friends out of mischief while their folks start putting things back to order."

She blindly reached for a mug and concentrated on pouring coffee into it as Logan spoke. April was Maisy's granddaughter, and after a lifetime of poor health that had been reversed thanks to an operation earlier that year, was becoming quite a handful. She figured Riley—who'd been resourceful enough to find her way alone from Olympia to the island—was probably equal to the task. "What about the, um, the ferry?"

"Two of Diego's boats sank. The third needs major repairs. The Coast Guard has already been out; picked up the heart-attack victim and a couple other injuries to transport them to the mainland."

"Then we could get another charter out here."

He shook his head. "The coastline is fogged in. Flights are grounded. The guard will be back with some supplies when they can, but they're dealing with other problems that are considerably more their domain. Why are you so anxious to get rid of Riley?"

Coffee sloshed over the side of her mug. "*You* came to the island to get her."

"That's not an answer."

Annie ripped a paper towel from the roll and sopped up the spill. "She's safer with Will and Noelle."

"Are you so sure about that?"

The towel crumpled in her fist. "You've been here

less than twenty-four hours, Logan. And look at all that's happened in that time.''

He leaned his elbows on the breakfast counter and his shoulders strained against the wrinkled fabric of his shirt. His expression was unreadable. ''I'll be as happy to get off this rock as anyone. But there's been a storm. Nobody's fault but nature's. Riley is fine. And nobody is any closer to knowing the real reason she ran away. So what's the hurry?''

She dropped the balled paper in the trash as she took a sip of the coffee. It nearly scorched through the roof of her mouth.

''It's hot,'' Logan offered blandly.

She let out an exasperated breath. ''Gee. Thanks for the warning.''

The corner of his lips tilted. ''Anytime.''

Her stomach was in knots and thanks to her tumbles the previous day, her body ached nearly everywhere. Yet she found herself struggling not to smile at him.

She didn't want to like Logan Drake. She'd liked him years ago. Too much. But that period of her life was so full of painful memories that anyone from it— including him—seemed tainted with it.

All of which was moot. The only thing that mattered right now was getting Riley back home—away from Annie—before something even worse happened. *That* was the hurry, she silently reminded herself.

She gingerly sipped the coffee, hoping it would dissolve the pained lump in her throat. All she succeeded in doing was burning her tongue.

''Annie.''

She glanced at Logan. It was all she dared. Then she looked back down into the strong black coffee steaming inside the mug. Still too hot to drink, but at least holding the mug warmed her cold hands. "I don't think it's ever been this cold since I've lived here."

"It's in the low 40's, probably. Thanks to the generator, everybody in the big building was warm, though. Including Riley. Sam doesn't have a clue when the power will be restored. Half the plant's fried. Looked like it took a hit of lightning."

She nodded. Tried to drink a little more, but contented herself more with inhaling the heated aroma. "I'm glad she was warm there, then."

"Thanks for the bed last night."

Her cheeks warmed, right along with her palms around the mug. "I, um, you're welcome."

"Not that I gave you much choice."

"True." She chanced another look at him, only to find herself unable to look away when his gaze captured hers. He still had that thin black ring surrounding his irises, making the blue seem even bluer.

"I was interested."

"Excuse me?"

"Last night. You said I wasn't interested. I was. And you knew it."

Her mouth ran dry.

"When you were seventeen." He pushed off the barstool. "And now."

Her spine bumped the refrigerator when he rounded the counter, seeming to take up all the space in her minute kitchen. Panic and something else—something she desperately feared was longing—streaked through her veins.

Longing? She didn't long for anything. She didn't allow herself that luxury.

"Stop!" She put out her arm, splaying her fingers against his chest. "I, um, I don't do this."

He raised an eyebrow. "Ever?"

"Never. And I don't believe you about…about before."

His lips twisted. "Right." He covered her fingers with his, pressing them over the heavy beat of his heart. "Feel that? Nothing's changed."

She swallowed. She couldn't have spoken just then to save her soul.

Despite the blur of beard, his jaw looked tight. "I thought I could clear my conscience. About this, at least."

His conscience? "I don't…Logan, I—"

"Hell," he whispered. Then covered her mouth with his.

Her mind went blank. Her nerves came alive.

A dream was one thing.

Reality another.

Not hell, she thought vaguely. *Heaven.*

Flavored with the heady taste of dark coffee. Textured with the soft rasp of an unshaven cheek against the palm of her hand. Protected by shoulders that she knew were wide enough to hold the world at bay.

Just that easily, that rapidly, she wanted to drown in it. Drown in his kiss. In his touch. But she couldn't. Oh, she couldn't. She'd shut off that part of her, hadn't she? Cut it out of her existence, because it was so much safer.

His arm slid behind her back, pulling her closer, keeping her upright when her knees dissolved, setting her coffee mug aside when she was in danger of dropping it. She shivered, a trembling that had nothing to do with the temperature and everything to do with his fingertips, slipping beneath her layers of fleece, grazing her spine. "Logan—"

"Sshh." He tightened his arms around her, and she sucked in a harsh breath as he lifted her and settled her on the counter, stepping between her legs, capturing her face gently between his hands, turning her lips up to his yet again.

Her head swam. Was this another dream? So exquisitely vivid that waking from it was almost painful? She dragged her mouth from his, pressing her forehead against his jaw.

This is real. He is real.

She wasn't hallucinating, she wasn't losing her mind.

She brushed her fingertips over his cheek and her fingers tingled. Then she pulled back from him. "No." Her breath was ragged. "Riley…I have to think about my…Riley."

His hands swept down her back, then up again, curving over her shoulders. "I told you. Maisy's keeping her busy. Believe me, if anyone can keep your niece in hand, it's her."

"No." She suddenly wriggled out of his hold, nearly scrambling off the counter. If she didn't move away from him now, she feared she wouldn't do so at all. "I can't. I won't. I'm not like that. I'm not…not Easy-A anymore."

His eyes narrowed. "You were never easy."

She'd tried so hard, for so many years to erase that part of her life. And she'd thought she'd succeeded. Except for those sly dreams that still tormented her sleep when she least expected it. Dreams of a night that had never happened. Not with him. Not with anyone she wanted to remember. They were only a defense against a reality she hated.

She pushed at her hair, realizing it had come loose from the clip.

"I...have to clean up. Have to, uh, start getting things back in order." Order is what she wanted. What she craved.

Logan shoved his hands in his pockets rather than reach for her when Annie sidled away from him, panic glazing her eyes from mossy to emerald. She looked like some fey creature seeking escape.

He shouldn't have kissed her. He knew it. But he sure in hell hadn't expected a reaction like this. "We will," he said cautiously. "The hot water on the camp stove is for you."

She was visibly trembling. "G-good." But she didn't move toward it, and he figured it was just as well, given the state she was in.

"I'll move it for you."

Her brows drew together. "What?"

"There's not enough for a real bath, but you can wash up with it. I'll pour it in the sink in the bathroom. You can add a little cold water to it so you don't burn yourself."

He watched her watch him as he suited his calm, steady words with action. And her wariness made something inside him hurt.

"Thank you." Her words were nearly silent when he'd dumped the boiling water into the sink. The steam from it billowed up, clouding the mirror above it. Then she quietly closed the bathroom door, leaving him standing in the narrow hallway with an oversized pan clenched in his hand.

He let out a long breath and stared at the smooth-paneled door. The door wasn't substantial. But he couldn't hear a single sound from inside. Not the splash of water, not the shifting of a rubber-soled sock or the rustle of too-large clothing designed to hide a slender, female body.

Too easily, he pictured her standing there in front of the sink, her eyes shadowed and turned inward, her body braced against the shudders that wracked it.

He knew what it was like to have demons in your mind. He recognized the signs. He'd battled his own— sometimes winning, too often losing.

But what demons were keeping company with Annie Hess?

He was beginning to suspect what they were. And the suspicion that somebody, somewhere along the line, had hurt Annie in ways no person deserved made him feel murderous.

He drew in a long breath. Exhaled in even longer, measured beats. But the feeling didn't pass.

It scared the hell out of him.

Chapter Eight

"What do you know about Annie?"

Logan was working alongside Sam Vega as they cleared the southern end of the main road of the trees that had fallen across it.

At the question, Sam straightened and ran his arm across his sweaty brow. He shrugged. "What's there to know? She keeps to herself and she's in business with your sister, man."

But Logan couldn't reach Sara, since the phone lines were still down. It was bad enough that he'd hadn't spoken with her in years. Then to pump her for information about Annie?

He frowned and swung the ax again, biting into another tree branch. "Turnabout is as bloody backward as it ever was," he muttered. "Not one single person has a chainsaw." He'd seen a house with a satellite dish, but did anyone have a chainsaw? Hell no.

They couldn't even use Sam's truck at this point to drag the trees, because they were caught awkwardly between the fence that strangled the road. Using the truck now would probably pull down the iron fence as well. And God knew nobody could touch the fence that cordoned off the property of the Castillo house.

The place was a sacred—albeit barren—cow to the Turns.

He glared at the fence. The trees. The rundown dwelling that sat beyond it on a cliff. "Backwards."

Sam grinned faintly. "Place is still a couple decades behind the times in some ways. There *are* folks who like it that way."

Logan grimaced and kept chopping. He wasn't one of them. "You must. You came back."

"Not to take a step backward in time or technology."

The branch finally groaned, tilting away from the main trunk. He kicked his boot against it, finishing the job, then dragged it away from the fence. Straightening, he tilted his head back, looking up at the sky. Over the course of the afternoon, it had cleared, and was as pristine blue as he ever remembered seeing it during his childhood. "Fickle weather."

Sam snorted softly. "Almost as bad as a woman. But in this instance—" he cast his gaze around "—I'm glad for the respite. We don't have the resources to get through one disaster, much less having another storm on top of it. Help me here. I think we've cut enough." He gestured at the heavy tree trunk.

Logan added his muscle, and, between the two of them, they managed to drag it—roots protruding up in the air like some maniacal hand out of a horror flick—

beyond the iron fence. When they'd cleared the fence, Sam used the winch on his truck to finish the job, dragging the tree clear of the road. Which left only two more trees to go.

Logan picked up the ax again and approached the next tree. The afternoon air was cold, crisp and smelled of fresh-cut wood. It was a combination completely out of place for Turnabout. If anything, it reminded him of Washington state. About the time of year that Will had been getting hitched.

He swung the ax, cutting off that particular thought. Beside him, Sam swung also. Wood chips flew as they fell into a rhythm and they steadily hacked their way through the next tree, then started on the last.

Logan's back began to ache. They'd both shrugged off their jackets despite the brisk temperature. Sam had long sent his brother Leo off for a saw, but the guy had yet to return. Obviously, Leo had taken to heart the Turn's typically fluid definition of *time*.

"I hate this," Logan muttered. The last tree was enormous. Had probably stood as a sentinel to the southern end of the island for over a hundred years. "It'd be easier to swim to the mainland and get a chainsaw." He looked at Sam. "Why'd you come back here?"

Sam grimaced, leaving the ax-head buried in the wood. "Why did you?"

"I'm not back."

Sam smiled faintly and uncapped the jug of water he'd brought, along with the miserably insufficient axes. The jug was nearly empty. "But you're here," he pointed out, slanting a look his way.

"Stuck here. For now."

Sam just shook his head and finished off the water. "That's what we all say."

"There's nothing on this island for me." Logan looked around at the landscape. Some of it was wild. Unkempt. With treacherous cliffs and barren ground. And then, a half mile up the road, a person could stand in the checkerboard of Annie and Sara's fields. They currently looked bedraggled, but even he could tell they were ordinarily lush with good health.

"Ask not what the island has for you but what you have for the island."

He wished he had a chainsaw is what he wished. "You getting philosophical in your old age?"

Sam grunted, his grin fading. "Watch it. I'll throw you in the tank. You got something going with Annie? That why you're asking about her?"

"No." The only thing he had going with Annie was a long-ago night that should never have occurred and newly acquired suspicions that would be just one more thing to keep him awake at night.

"Heard you spent the night at her place."

"People around here always were too nosy."

"Small towns," Sam said. "Nothing more interesting to speculate over than what the neighbors are doing behind closed doors."

"And you came back to it."

Sam tossed the empty jug beyond the fence and it sailed into the back of his truck. "There are worse things."

For a long time, Logan had doubted that. Until he began dwelling in the worst the world had to offer. He flexed his back. Then his hands. Grabbed the long handle again and continued chopping.

The irony of his task didn't escape him. Once again, he was cleaning up a mess. This one just happened to be caused by the destruction of nature, rather than the destruction of man.

Just once, he thought, he'd like to make something new.

"Whoa. Wicked trees."

Both men looked up from their task at the young voice.

Logan absorbed the sight of Annie followed by Riley move slowly toward the tree. Annie had changed into jeans since that morning, but still looked as if she were drowning in layers of knit sweaters. Her niece was similarly dressed. It was almost like having double vision.

"Hey, Annie," Sam called out easily. "Don't think even your talents can save these babies."

Annie and Riley stopped on the other side of the last tree wedged between the road and the fence. Even lying on the ground the branches soared over their heads. Her gaze on the tree, Annie set down the bucket she was carrying and slowly settled her palm on a thick, gnarled branch. "What a shame." She didn't look Logan's way.

He watched her hand. Her thumb stroked gently against the bark.

"Oh, man. People really carve their initials into trees?" Riley had scrambled into the thick of the branches and was peering at the trunk. "With hearts and everything. That is *so* corny."

Logan deliberately looked away from Annie's gentle caress of the uprooted tree. Despite Riley's bored tone, she was avidly studying the etchings that marred the tree trunk. "Some of those carvings are pretty old," he said. "When corny was *in*."

"Logan's probably got an initial or two on there," Sam said. "He was always bringing girls up here to—"

"Watch the sunsets," Logan inserted.

Sam's lips twitched. "Right."

"And I usually ran into you and your flavor of the day when I got here," Logan reminded the other man, amused at the memory. He'd almost forgotten that there had been some decent times on Turnabout.

"That's just gross."

"Glad you think so," Annie smoothly told Riley. "Then I don't have to worry about you and your new friend from Denver watching any *sunsets,* do I?"

Logan caught the look between the two females. "Friend?"

"Yeah, a friend." Riley's voice was defensive.

"Kenny Hobbes," Annie said. "His family are guests at Maisy's. They seemed to have…hit it off." Her expression was anything but delighted.

Riley huffed and deliberately pushed aside a branch. "Nobody carved their whole name. There are only initials. Look at this one."

Logan waited, wondering if Annie would pursue the issue. But after a moment her shoulders relaxed and she moved over beside Riley, slipping between two branches to see. "HD and CC. The heart around them is really elaborate." She touched the bulging bark surrounding the carved sentiment. "Look at the way the tree's healed around it."

"I bet this one's been here longer." Riley poked at another carving, higher up the trunk. It was far more faded. "Looks like ES and...what is that? Something, then a C."

"Probably an L," Sam said. "Luis Castillo. He was the son of the people who built this old place. Supposedly, the Turnabout curse started because Luis was betrayed by his fiancée Elena when she fell in love with a friend of his he'd brought to the island after the First World War."

Riley snorted. "A curse? What kind of idiot believes in curses?"

An island of them, Logan thought. He studied the HD and CC for a moment.

"Sara believes it," Annie said. "Maisy believes it. Neither of them are *idiots*."

"They'd be better off if they didn't believe," Logan said flatly. "Riley's right. Superstitious nonsense is what it is."

Annie's eyes—looking as green now as the leaves still clinging to the tree branches surrounding her—looked at him. "Your father says the same thing. But a person *does* wonder."

Being in agreement with Hugo was nothing Logan strove to obtain. "Do you even know what the curse claims? Turns hardly used to talk about it, because they were too freaked it'd mar their lives." He doubted things on that score had changed much.

"Sara told me."

"She did?" Sam looked surprised.

"Well...what is it?" Riley looked impatient.

"It's garbage," Logan said.

Annie's chin lifted a little. "What are you worried about, Logan? You told me yourself you're not a Turn and we all know you can't wait to leave the island again.''

"Doesn't matter what my plans are," Logan countered. "Somebody should either restore Castillo House or tear it down."

Annie blinked a little, and looked at her niece.

Riley just lifted her eyebrows. "I said the same thing when she—'' her chin jerked toward her aunt "—said we were coming out here to rescue some of her plants. The place is a dump."

"Well, anyway," Annie said hurried, "Luis Castillo's fiancée married his friend, Jonathan, who was a stranger to the island. Luis was brokenhearted, and as a result, his mother cast a curse that people born on the island would only find happiness with someone else born on the island, apparently to prevent something like what Elena had done—marrying an outsider."

Riley made a face. "Weird."

"Actually, what I think is interesting is that *since* then, supposedly, nothing grows in the ground around Castillo House. Sara says it was the price the Castillo family paid in return for the curse." Annie glanced beyond Logan to the property surrounding the decaying house. "The trees were the only living things left, but they stood here at the edge of the property next to the fence. That's why I tried planting near them."

"There used to be an iron gate that blocked off the road," Sam said. "But I finally removed it because it was getting too dangerous for the kids who came out here and played on it. If the gate were still here, the trees would actually have been on the outside of it."

"Are those your plants?" Riley pointed at a sparse

row along the fence line. The stems were barely strong enough to hold a leaf. "*That's* what we are supposed to save?"

Annie nodded. "There's no physical reason why plants shouldn't thrive here. It's, well, it is *weird.*"

"It's probably some Turn who dumped something toxic around the place to prove their point that the curse existed," Logan countered. "And the trees are so old, the root systems were too deep to be affected."

Her gaze slanted his way, amused. "Skeptic."

"Realist."

"Well, as it happens, I've had the soil tested and it's perfectly fine. A little acidic, but not unusually so."

"So, why does it matter to you whether or not you can get plants to grow out here?"

"Oh, I will," she said, her voice determined. "I can grow plants anywhere. But this space is perfect to expand our fields for Island Botanica. Sara and I need more land to produce more crops to keep up with our mail-order business. The thing that makes our products unique is that everything is derived from plants grown here on Turnabout. We're totally organic, totally pure. And we don't want to have to obtain supplies off island."

She was serious.

He looked over his shoulder at the barren expanse surrounding the house that—as far as he was concerned—was pretty much an eyesore. "Is the property even available?" The last member of the Castillo family had left the island when he was a baby. He figured he'd have heard by now—given the grapevine—if a Castillo had ever returned. That would have been major news for Turnabout.

"Sara's been looking into it. That's one of the reasons she's in San Diego this past week. Doing some title research on the land. The last owner of record was Caroline Castillo, but we haven't been able to locate her, yet. She left Turnabout nearly forty years ago. We're not even sure she's still alive. It'd be easier if we could afford an investigator to do research, but we're getting there. Slowly," she added with a wry shrug.

Logan picked up the ax and moved around to the top of the tree, away from where Annie and Riley stood.

"Isn't there some way we could at least save the tree trunk?" Annie's voice stopped him midswing.

"For what?"

"I don't know. Posterity. These old carvings meant something to people." She gestured toward the other trees. "Look at all that. It's not as if you need *this* one for firewood."

"If we don't get the power restored soon, we might," Sam said. He looked back at the tree. "Where would we put it?"

"I don't know. The community center or something. The town council could decide, right? I'll keep the trunk in my workshop if nobody else wants it. Think about it, Sam. This tree was probably the oldest living thing on Turnabout."

Sam shrugged and looked at Logan, his expression not at all convinced. "We'll see. For now, let's just get it out of the road." He caught Riley's arm and helped her climb over the trunk, then handed her the shovel she'd been carrying.

Annie followed but stopped short, wincing. "Hold

on, Riley, I'm—ouch!—caught." She twisted, reaching behind her.

Logan stepped through the branches toward her. "Stop moving." He worked his way around behind her. "Your sweater is hung up on a branch." He reached for the broken branch that snagged her, and felt a fine shiver dance down her spine as he worked the sweater free. "Did it scratch you?"

"No." She looked up at him, then away. "Yes. But it's okay." Her soft lips pressed together.

Heat blasted through him.

If she moved an inch, she'd be pressed up against him. He wedged his arm between Annie and the branches, giving them both more breathing room. The last thing he needed was to send her back into a panic, and finding out he was hard just from looking at her face would probably do just that. "Be careful."

Her gaze skidded over his face, lingering on his mouth. "I will. Um…thanks."

"Talk to Hugo."

"What? It's just a scratch, Logan. I hardly need a doctor's opinion. I have my own remedies, anyway. Aloe vera is very—"

"About Caroline Castillo."

"Oh." She blinked. "Right. Your dad would have known her, of course. He hasn't said anything special to Sara, though."

She shifted and despite multiple layers of knit, he felt the soft push of her breasts against his side. "I'm not surprised. Sara doesn't know."

"Know what?"

He tapped the inscription on the trunk once. "Caroline Castillo left Turnabout when her affair with my father came to light. Wouldn't surprise me if Hugo kept track of her.'' It's what his mother had always believed. Her suspicions had dogged her into misery for most of Logan's childhood. Every time Hugo had left the island, she'd ranted that he'd gone to see his lover. As far as Logan knew, Hugo had never denied it.

Her eyes were soft, her expression shocked. "I'm sorry."

"It's old news."

"Sometimes it's hard to acknowledge that your parents aren't perfect. But Logan, that was a *long* time ago. If that's what's causing the distance between the two of you, then—"

"Hey." Riley waved the shovel handle through the branches and they rustled, leaves cascading everywhere. "You better not be looking for any *sunsets* in there."

Amusement tugged at him. The girl really was protective of her aunt. He wondered if either one of them noticed it.

Annie's cheeks had flushed. "Thanks for the, uh, the rescue. Yet another one. And for helping save the tree trunk. You're a good guy, Logan Drake."

His amusement died.

Logan could detest his father for his mother's unhappiness all he wanted. But Hugo had still done some decent things. He'd been the only doctor the island possessed.

The truth of it was that Hugo was closer to being a "good guy" than Logan was.

"No," he said so softly she'd never hear as she worked her way from the clinging branches. "I'm not."

Chapter Nine

Logan sat in the sheriff's office. Even after darkness fell, he didn't light the utilitarian lantern sitting on Sam's desk as he thumbed the mike to the emergency radio that Sam had managed to procure. "Any more letters?"

For a moment, his only answer was static. Then Will's voice came on again. "Not for a week now. I can send a charter out for you and Riley."

Logan stared at the microphone. There was no reason for Will not to do exactly that. But there was an itch at the base of his spine that told him to wait. Wait.

How many times had he sat in some filth-encrusted location, his finger hovering on a trigger, his eye on a scope, as that same itch told him to wait. Wait.

When he'd been in Will's office that day, the other man had shown him a file of letters containing oblique threats to the effect that if he didn't back out of the special election for attorney general, he'd regret it. The letters hadn't been directly threatening, but they'd been worrying enough that Will hadn't been as anxious as he might otherwise have been to get Riley back under his roof.

Will hadn't liked the idea of his daughter seeking out Annie, but until he had a finger on the source of the threatening letters, he'd also figured she was just as safe *away* from Olympia.

Logan's thoughts raced, ranging from the meeting he'd had with Will and Cole when he'd been asked to come after Riley, to keep watch over her, to bring her home when they all deemed it safe, to Annie.

He thumbed the mike. "Wait."

Static met him again.

Though it had been sixteen years since they'd been in the same place at the same time, Logan knew Will was worried about Riley. The man was in an untenable situation.

Wanting his daughter back.

Wanting her safe, even more.

His old friend was undoubtedly going to be the next attorney general for Washington state. He could have depended on any number of more traditional means for retrieving his daughter since he, himself, was embroiled in the middle of a special election. But he hadn't. And Logan still had trouble adjusting his cynicism enough to believe that Will's decision hadn't been affected—at least in part—by the adverse effect on the polls if it came to public awareness that his only daughter had run away from home.

So Will had prevailed upon his connection with

Coleman Black, who in turn, had put Logan on the task. The only one of the three men who hadn't seemed surprised by the pairing had been Cole. Which probably meant his boss had an ulterior motive in bringing two guys who'd lost touch over the years back in contact.

He finally received a static-laden answer. "Check in tomorrow."

Logan let go of the mike and sat back in Sam's desk chair, scrubbing his hands down his face.

He knew his reasons for putting Will off were more selfish than not, despite that faint itch of his. But he wasn't ready to haul Riley back home, not without somebody figuring out what the hell had motivated her to run away in the first place. And he wasn't ready to leave Annie just yet, either. Not until…until *what?*

He shoved back the chair.

Cole would have a laugh if he saw Logan now. His cold-blooded clean-up man, troubled by people from a past that he'd long ago cut from his life.

Eventually, Logan left Sam's office and went to the community center where nearly the entire town was gathered, pooling food for dinner and anxiously awaiting a progress report on utilities and supplies. And again, he went through the ritual of responding to the "nice to see you back" comments that followed his progress before he spotted Annie sitting at a long table.

She was turned away from him, talking to someone at the next table. He watched her profile for a long moment. And when her glance turned his way and her eyes widened a little and the corners of her soft lips lifted in a faint smile, his heart stopped.

Hell.

He shook it off and walked over to her. "I got a message to Will that everyone here is okay." He set his bowl of chili on the long narrow table and sat down beside her. "Where's Riley?"

Her faint smile died. "I suppose Will said to get her home. Pronto."

"Nobody on the isle is going anywhere for the time being."

She chewed the corner of her lip for a moment, then seemed to accept his words. "She's at Maisy's again. She's pretty fascinated with April, apparently. And she, um, she's already eaten, so I didn't see the harm in it."

He'd only wondered where the girl was, not why Annie felt justified in letting the kid do what she wanted.

Hell, they *were* stuck on an island.

He began eating.

"Hi, Logan. Annie."

At the too-cheerful greeting, he sighed and looked up as Darla Towers slid into the empty seat across from them.

"This is such a nightmare, isn't it?" Darla crossed her arms on the table and leaned forward. "I'm going to die if I can't get a bottle of your lavender cream, Annie." Her words were for Annie but the woman's dark eyes were on him.

"We have plenty of cream at the shop, Darla. I'll get some to you."

"Thanks. Now if I could just find someone to help me put it on my back." She giggled.

"Try Leo," he suggested blandly.

Darla's lips tightened and she stood from the chair so quickly it nearly tipped over before she walked away.

"You could have been nicer, you know," Annie said a moment later.

Logan shrugged. He wasn't interested in Darla Towers. He wasn't interested in any woman on the island, save one. There had been plenty of women in his life, but not a one who'd kept him awake at night. Not like the memory of Annie Hess. He continued eating, perfectly aware that Annie was doing more toying with her spoon than using it to eat the soup that filled her bowl.

The community center was noisy with chatter. Several people stopped by to ask Annie about her shop, or to offer assistance with the fields if she needed it. The only person who hadn't stopped by was Hugo. He was there, all right, over in the corner of the community center with his medical bag and a table of first-aid supplies. Judging by the look of it, he'd been wrapping, swabbing and icing since long before Logan arrived for dinner.

And, as well as being aware of Annie's lack of appetite, he caught the surreptitious looks she cast his way, then Hugo's.

"Appearances are deceiving."

"What?"

He jerked his chin in the direction of his father. "You're sitting here wondering whether what I told you is true or not, because he looks like the saint of Turnabout over there."

"No," she said quietly, "I'm sitting here thinking how sad it is that there's such distance between the two of you."

He was amused, despite himself. "How long has it been since you talked with George and Lucia?"

Her head tilted, acknowledging the irony. "The situations aren't really the same, though. I know what you said about…about Dr. Hugo, but as I've said, it was a long time ago. Caroline Castillo left the island decades ago. You said yourself that you were a baby."

"Yet the ripples of that Castillo rock falling into the Drake pond continued for a long time," he said evenly. "Eat your soup."

She looked down at the spoon she was swirling in her bowl, as if surprised that it was still there. Then he felt the whisper of her gaze lingering on him.

He finally pushed away his bowl of chili and looked right at her. "What?"

She frowned a little. "What *have* you been doing all these years, Logan?"

"I told you. Consulting."

"For whom?"

"You wouldn't have heard of them."

"Try me."

He lifted an eyebrow, giving her words an entirely different meaning than she'd intended.

The pupils of her eyes suddenly dilated, and she moistened her lips, looking away. "Is it in law? This consulting you do?" Her voice sounded a little strangled.

"More or less."

She folded her hands together. "Are you *trying* to make me more curious about you, Logan? Or is this just all part of that hardness that you hide underneath a veil of civility?"

Their gazes tangled, breaking only when the chatter

around them suddenly ceased. Annie looked away from him, her cheeks flushed.

It was Sam, now standing on a small riser, who had garnered everyone's attention.

Logan listened with half an ear as the sheriff read off a brief series of announcements that met with an equal number of groans from the residents. Most of his attention, however, was on Annie's assessment of him.

Coming from anyone else, it would have rolled off his back. From her, though, it didn't.

He heard Annie sigh when Sam was finished speaking. "I don't know how to live without electricity," she murmured.

The ironies continued. "Fortunately," he said, "I do."

Annie's curiosity where Logan was concerned was still unquenched when she tracked down her niece after dinner and steered her back to the beach house.

Logan hadn't accompanied them. She'd told herself she was glad. Once home, she lit several candles and started boiling water on the camp stove. If it took her all night, she was going to boil enough water to provide Riley and herself with decent baths.

She learned a few hours later, however, that the fuel for the stove only went so far. Riley got her bath.

Annie did not.

Which meant that she had yet to fully wash away the grime from their efforts earlier that day on the Castillo property. With Riley's help, she'd removed two flats of the small plants that had been beaten down by the rain so badly they'd barely clung to the soil. The flats now sat on the floor next to Annie's couch.

When the sun came up in the morning, she'd move them next to the glass door, to catch the light. Right now, they were warmer away from the window.

Riley shuffled into the room, her hair hidden beneath a towel. "The candle in the bathroom's going out. It's burned down to nothing."

"Logan said he'd get more candles when he gets the batteries for your Walkman." He'd disappeared after the community potluck dinner, saying only that he'd bring some supplies back to her house later.

She wondered if that meant he intended to sleep here again.

She wondered what she'd tell him if he did.

"If there are any batteries and stuff *left*." Riley's glum voice interrupted Annie's unnerving thoughts. "Everything's getting used up so fast."

"Well, I can't help with batteries. But I'm not worried about candles. We'll pull them from the stock at the shop if necessary." She studied Riley for a moment. "Guess you didn't count on having to play frontier woman when you came here."

Riley snorted. "Just 'cause I wish we had the electricity back doesn't mean I want to go home." She crouched down next to the plants, pushing up the sleeves of the sweatshirt Annie had given her to wear; the supply of clothes she'd carried with her in her backpack had been meager.

Since Annie wore her clothing too large in the first place, her niece was practically swimming in the garment. Without her customary globs of eyeliner and mascara and in the too-large sweatshirt, Riley looked just as young as she really was.

Which was way too young to have made her way, alone, from Washington state to Turnabout. It was a miracle that she'd managed it without encountering any trouble.

Annie swallowed down the panic over those awful what-ifs. "The Coast Guard will be coming by in the next day or two, Riley. The sheriff thinks he can arrange it for you and Logan to go with them to the mainland." She moistened her lips. She hadn't told Logan about her conversation with Sam, but he'd surely agree. "I think you should go."

"Fine. I'll go to the mainland."

She pressed her hand against her midriff, willing away a surge of dizziness before it occurred to her— just as rapidly—that Riley's answer had come entirely too easily. She narrowed her eyes, studying her niece's stiff shoulders. "To the mainland—but not *home*."

Riley didn't reply.

Annie shoved her hair more securely into the clip at the back of her head. She sat down beside her niece, casting about for something helpful to say, some magic words to make everything right. "You know, Riley, there's nothing you…can't tell your parents…that you can't tell me." Maybe if she'd had someone in her life who'd seemed interested in listening to her, things for Annie might have turned out differently.

Riley shot to her feet. "I'm going to bed."

Annie sighed. "Goodnight."

But the girl had already left the room. A moment later, she heard the bedroom door close.

Feeling older than she ought to, Annie slowly stood.

She went into the kitchen. Checked the phone even though she knew it was futile.

Nothing but silence filled her house.

Annie wasn't one to constantly need the noise of a television or a radio around her. But still, the utter silence was unnerving, possibly because there was nothing to blot out the voices in her head.

She finally grabbed one of the pots she'd used to boil water for Riley's bath and stuck it under the tap, filling it again. She grabbed a towel and washcloth and a bottle of Island Botanica shampoo, and let herself out the rear door.

Ahh, yes. The sound of the ocean, quiet though it was, filled the air. For a long moment she stood there on her deck and absorbed the peaceful sound, before carrying everything down to the fire pit. She made another trip back to the house, sorting through the wood pile for the driest pieces, which she also carried back to the pit. It took a few attempts, but she finally managed to get a flame going, and once the fire caught and burned brightly, she set the pot of water on the blackened grill that was suspended over one edge.

She left the water to heat, and traipsed back up to the house. She filled the empty water jug, grabbed another towel and her robe, stuck some toiletries in the robe's pocket, then stopped by Riley's bedroom door. She knocked softly and when there was no answer, her heart jerked in her chest. Riley had been exhausted, she assured herself. She wouldn't have sneaked out again.

Still, Annie opened the door and peeked inside. Her niece was sprawled on the bed, face turned away from the door.

Annie pressed her forehead against the door for a long moment, waiting for her heart to climb down from her throat. Then she started to close the door once more, but stopped. She set the water jug on the floor and went inside the room to carefully draw the quilt over Riley.

The sleeping girl didn't stir and Annie quietly left the room again. She picked up the water and headed back outside.

Only when she stopped shaking a long while later did she get around to the task of bathing. She spread one towel on the wide concrete edge surrounding the pit and slid out of her clothes, working in shifts, because it was simply too cold to completely disrobe all at once.

She wasn't afraid of being seen. There were only stars to see whatever she did on this little stretch of beach and she knew she could dance naked under the moon if she chose without anyone knowing. A bath was her only intention, though, and she made quick work of it.

The water in the pot was too hot and the water in the jug was too cold for the process to be enjoyable. Within minutes, she had her damp body wrapped in her robe and she set about the task of washing her hair. By the time she poured the last of the jug's contents over her head to finish rinsing her hair, she was shivering so badly she ached from it.

She wrapped her head in the towel and left everything but the bottle of her lavender cream right there on the sand as she jogged back toward the house, leaving the glowing embers of the flame to burn themselves out.

But the glow of another ember stopped her in her tracks as she made it to the deck. "Logan? Is that you?"

"Sorry. Didn't mean to startle you." He sat on the edge of the deck, and he leaned forward into the thin gleam of moonlight to snuff out his cigarette in the sand.

Embarrassment joined her shivering, increasing her discomfort tenfold. She'd expected him to take longer, if he'd return that night at all.

How long had he been sitting there?

It didn't matter how long, she assured herself. The fire pit was too far from the house to see anything. Even if he'd been in the house, or on the deck, he couldn't have seen her hasty, hunched-against-the-cold nudity.

Are you sure, Annie? Or had you hoped he would? You knew he'd eventually come back to the house. He'd promised to bring by more supplies. You're still the same as you always were, aren't you?

The voice in her head had always been colored with her mother's judgmental tone.

"Annie?" Logan's voice seemed to come at her through a fog. "Are you okay?"

Chapter Ten

Logan started to stand. Annie looked as if she was ready to collapse. But she blinked. Waved her hand a little and tugged the lapels of her robe closer together. "I'm fine. You just…surprised me. I, um, I didn't know you smoked."

"I try not to." Smoking was one of those things that tended to give away your presence.

"Oh. Well. I was just washing my hair."

"So I see."

She stepped up on the deck and edged closer to the door, wiping sand from her feet as she did so.

"I brought the candles and batteries."

"Good." Her response was a little too quick. "Riley will be relieved. She has one of those portable CD players."

"I know. She told me earlier."

"Right." She smiled weakly and tugged on her belt again.

She was obviously uncomfortable.

"I also brought more fuel for the stove," he said. "The store's nearly out; you'll probably want to save it for necessities."

"Which probably doesn't include using it all to heat water so Riley can have a warm bath."

"Probably not," he agreed, knowing full well that was what she'd already done. "I would have brought you a lantern, but there aren't any mantles left in the store. I would've gotten you a gas grill for cooking, but propane's all sold out, too."

"How much did you spend? I'll pay you—"

"Forget about it. You're shivering. Go inside."

She reached for the door and slid it open. "Are you...where are you...Riley's asleep in her room. I think she's dead to the world for once."

"Glad to hear it. Chasing after her yesterday was more than enough for me."

Annie still didn't go inside. "What I meant is that her bedroom isn't available tonight. But the couch is. If you need a place to sleep that is. It's pretty comfortable. I'm not sure it's long enough for you. And you'd probably be warmer over at the community center. Or there might be someone else's house where you'd prefer to stay." She pressed her lips together, seeming to realize she was babbling.

"Are you trying to talk me into or out of using your couch?"

"Good question." She hesitated for a moment. "I, um, I don't want a repeat of what happened this morning."

It was an unpalatable nugget, but not an unexpected one. "Neither do I." He didn't think he could stand seeing her scramble away from him again the way she had.

"Okay then. Well, it's up to you. About the couch, I mean." She went inside and closed the door. She didn't lock it, though.

He let out a rough breath and pulled another cigarette from the pack he'd picked up along with the candles, the batteries, the fuel.

He bent his head against the breeze to light it, then sat there on the edge of the deck, his feet planted in the sand. Behind him, the plastic covering the window over her sink rippled, shifting and sighing with the wind.

In front of him, not quite out of his line of sight, was the glow from Annie's dying fire and beyond that, miles of night-dark ocean. Always there. Never silent. Never the same, yet never different.

He'd been on the island for two days. Long enough for the expected urge to leave it again to grab hold of him.

Yet behind him, inside a small beach cottage that had been built so long ago he remembered it from his own childhood, lived a woman who had got under his skin as easily as she ever had.

It wasn't the island that was causing his restlessness now, he knew. It was Annie.

Maybe—as unlikely as it might seem to him—she *didn't* remember what had happened between them all those years ago. But he sure as hell did. And of all the things he'd done in his life that he regretted, that night was the worst.

He sat there until his cigarette burned down into one long ash, until clouds rolled in and obliterated the thin moonlight, until the only noise coming from the house behind him was the hissing ripple of thick plastic.

Sam had offered him a bed for as long as he needed it. Given Annie's obvious discomfort and his own state of mind, taking him up on the offer was the wise choice.

He snuffed and stripped the cigarette out of habit, then pushed to his feet and silently slid open the glass door.

"I wasn't putting on a show out there at the fire pit for you." Her voice came out of the darkness the moment he stepped inside, and he went still.

"I thought you'd be in bed by now."

"Obviously, I'm not." He heard the scrape of a match, then watched her light the candle sitting on the coffee table in front of her. "I don't know what you saw, or think you saw, but *I* thought I was alone," she said. "So, if you want someone to strip for you, I suggest you look elsewhere."

Even in the minimal light cast by the candle, he could see the stiffness in her posture. The protective way she clutched her robe around her.

The fact was, he'd seen every furtive movement she'd made down there by the fire pit. He'd seen the way sparks had danced up from the fire when she'd stoked it. He'd seen the way she'd revealed one leg, then the other in the orange fire glow. Washing. Drying. Quickly. He'd seen the graceful arch of her back when she'd tugged off her sweater.

There'd been nothing seductive in her actions. Only

simple practicality against the conditions in which they'd found themselves.

The sight had nevertheless grabbed him by the throat and yanked all the way down to his gut.

"Well?" Tension vibrated in her voice.

"I didn't see a thing," he lied.

The release of her tension was palpable. She cleared her throat. "Well…that's good. I, um, I'll get you a sheet and blanket for the couch, then. You…*are* planning to sleep here?"

"Yeah."

She quickly left the room. Returned a moment later with a neatly folded stack of bedding. "I hope you'll be warm enough."

"I don't think that'll be a problem." Fortunately, his self-directed irony escaped her.

"Okay."

She hovered close enough that he could smell the soft scent of her. And Annie seemed to have no clue as she stood there, unknowingly driving nails into his coffin of want. "Well. Good night, Logan."

If she didn't leave he was going to touch her, regardless of what they'd both said.

"I plan to wash up, myself, Annie," he said evenly. "With hot water. Right there in the kitchen next to the stove. So unless you want to see something *you* don't want to see, I suggest you stay in your room once you go there."

Her lips parted. She ran her hand down the hair she'd obviously braided while he'd sat out on the deck, as if she were actually contemplating his words.

She was killing him.

"Annie—"

She fled.

* * *

Another storm hit the island before morning.

An awesome crack of thunder jerked Annie upright in her bed. Before the second round finished rattling the windows, she'd thrown back the covers and left her room at a run.

Riley was sitting up in her bed when Annie darted into her room. "Great." The girl flopped back down. "I thought I was dreaming."

"Maybe it won't be as severe," Annie said hopefully. The window next to Riley's bed had no curtains. Lightning flickered outside, but not long enough to really illuminate anything.

"Good, 'cause I don't want to sleep in the bathtub." Riley yanked the quilt over her head.

"The resilience of youth."

Annie whirled around at Logan's soft comment. He stood near the door. A flash of lightning revealed enough of him to assure he hadn't been caught mid-bath. She knew that he'd had plenty of time to accomplish his ablutions, but that hadn't kept her from lying awake in her bed for the past few hours thinking about it.

"More resilient than I am," she murmured, moving past him into the hallway. He started to pull Riley's door closed, but she touched his arm, staying his movement.

He looked at her and she snatched back her hand. Curled her fingers safely against her palm. "I think we should leave it open."

"Not if you're gonna stand there talking about it all

night." Riley's voice was muffled by the quilt, but still clear.

It was too dark to see for certain, but Annie felt sure that Logan smiled. She headed back to the kitchen where she felt around—aided by the flickering lightning—for the matches she'd left near the candle. But Logan's hand covered the book of matches first and she heard the soft scrape, saw the bright flare, and in the glow of it found his gaze on her face.

She swallowed. In a blink, the moment passed. He lit the candle. Another crack of thunder had her wincing.

"I know it's the lightning that causes the damage, but I really *hate* that thunder." She kept her voice low, striving for normalcy. "Do you think we should stay here?"

"I don't particularly want to walk to town in the rain unless we have to."

"Too bad you gave back Leo's golf cart." Annie rubbed her arms. She'd jumped from bed too rapidly to think about grabbing her robe to cover her thick flannel pajamas, and she was excruciatingly aware of the fact that he wore only a pair of dark jeans.

She moved to the glass door and peered out. "It doesn't seem as windy, at least."

"Small mercies."

She looked back to see him moving to the couch, flexing his arm, as if it pained him, before he stretched out with a deep sigh. "Go back to sleep, Annie. I'll wake you up if the storm gets worse."

"I wasn't asleep."

"Go to bed anyway."

Still, she hesitated. "Your arm is hurting, isn't it? From that piece of roof that hit you from the shack."

"I'll live."

"Did the skin break?"

"It's fine, Annie. Go to bed."

"But I have some ointment that might help." It bothered her that she hadn't thought to ask before now. If it hadn't been for her and Riley, he would never have been near that decrepit shack in the first place. He wasn't indestructible. Of course he could have gotten hurt. "I just need to know if the skin is broken or not. Some remedies—"

"If I agree to use your goop will you go to bed?" He sounded exasperated.

"Yes."

"Fine." He hardly sounded agreeable.

Annie hurried into the bathroom and fumbled around in the dark cupboard beneath the sink until she found her plastic box of first-aid supplies. She carried it, along with a washcloth she wet under the faucet, out to the living room and sat down on the hassock in front of the couch, then flipped off the lid. "Sit up."

"I can do it."

She looked at him, the tube in her hand. "You took the hit on the back side of your shoulder."

"You still like to get your way, don't you?" He sat up and twisted around so she could reach the spot where he'd taken the brunt of the blow from the shack's roof.

She squirted out the ointment on her fingers and carefully spread it over his arm and the hard bulge of his shoulder. It heated gently as she worked it in, and she heard him sigh.

"Feel better?"

"That you're probably spreading pig placenta all over me?"

"Eye of newt," she corrected blandly.

He turned his head and looked at her.

"Cayenne," she relented. "And a few other things, but trust me. You don't want to get it near your eyes, or use this on broken skin. It'd burn like fury."

"Pepper." He shook his head. "Damnedest thing."

"It'll help, though. I promise. I could also make you an herbal tea. Healing from the inside is as critical—more so—than healing from the outside. A little valerian and passion flower, or maybe black willow and—"

"No thanks. Do you do chants, too? Maybe under your soft skin you're a Turn, after all. The original Castillos were supposedly into voodoo."

"Ergo, the curse."

"Right."

"Western medicine is the new kid on the block, Logan. Natural remedies have been around far longer."

"Well, my herbalist friend, for tonight we'll make do with the pepper goop on my arm." Amusement had replaced his exasperation.

It was ridiculous. Their conditions were not quite miserable, but another few days without utilities or the ability to reach the mainland, and they would be. Yet, Annie found herself smiling.

Mostly because Logan was smiling. A true smile. One that wasn't underlaid with that sense of grimness he carried around with him.

She capped the ointment tube and wiped her fingers

on the damp washcloth. Then she rose and left everything on the breakfast counter.

She still doubted that she'd sleep. But she *had* agreed. "Good night, Logan."

"Good night, Annie."

She padded down the dark hall to her room and climbed back into bed. Outside, thunder still crackled.

She pulled the blankets up to her neck and closed her eyes.

And finally slept.

Chapter Eleven

Three days on the island.

Logan stood in the road and eyed the colorful house. It had been converted into an office for Dr. Hugo Drake so long ago that he couldn't remember it ever being used *as* a house. The place hardly looked professional. Wind chimes hung from the eaves on the porch. How they'd managed to survive the storm, he didn't know. But then maybe his old man kept a bushel of wind chimes stored inside and he just hung up more of the infernal things when he wanted.

The front door was wide open. He went up the steps, ducking under the chimes, and went inside.

His father was with a patient.

Logan didn't learn that from the receptionist who sat at the battered desk in the front room. He knew it because he could hear the murmur of voices through the thin walls. Logan headed for a chair in the hall near Hugo's examining rooms. An upturned barrel was beside the chair. The barrel had sat there as long as he could remember, too.

There'd been a time when he'd sat on Hugo's knee while they played solitaire on top of the barrel.

He shoved his hands in his pockets and looked out the door that was open at the rear of the building. He could see the rooftop of Maisy's Place, the tall spires of palm trees clustered around it. And beyond that, the glitter of water.

His gaze went back to the barrel. So many things were just the way he remembered, the way he expected.

Unexpected, though, was the small, inexpertly carved box that sat on top of the barrel.

The carvings on the sides and top weren't perfect. But the wood was smooth as he ran his thumb back and forth over it, and the lid—when he pushed experimentally on it—still fitted securely.

He'd made the thing in the sixth grade. During wood shop. Back when his mother was still alive. He lifted the lid. A thumb-worn deck of playing cards was stored inside.

He closed the box and left it on the barrel, and then headed back to the reception area.

Hugo stood near the now-vacant desk in conversation with his patient. Other than a glance, he gave no indication what he thought about Logan's appearance, until his business was concluded and he had been paid by his elderly female patient with a batch of her homemade plum preserves. He sat the jars of preserves on the desk, then studied his cold cigar for a moment before tucking it between his teeth. "Hear you've taken up with young Annie."

Logan stepped more fully into the waiting area. "She's past the age of consent." He was damned if he'd let the old man make him feel defensive. "What happened to Caroline?"

Hugo looked blank for a fraction of a second. Then his eyes narrowed. "Why are *you* interested? Now?"

"Sara and Annie want the Castillo House."

"They want the land around Castillo House," Hugo countered.

"Since you know that, why not help your daughter acquire it?"

"Lend her money?" Hugo's lips twisted as he picked up one of the jars sitting on the desk. "S'pose I could start selling off Mabel Bellanova's plum preserves." He set the jar down with a soft thump.

Logan wasn't amused. "By telling her how to reach Caroline."

Hugo looked weary. He sat down on the top of the desk. "She left the isle long before Sara was born. You were an infant. It's the last I saw of her."

"She was the love of your life."

Hugo's gaze met Logan's. "You telling or asking?"

"Stating a fact," Logan said flatly.

"A fact according to your mother."

"Well, I guess she'd have known."

Hugo's lips twisted. He said nothing.

"Where did she go after she left Turnabout?"

"I don't know."

"I don't believe you."

"And I can't help that, any more than I could ever change what your mother thought."

"What she *knew*."

"You're as pigheaded as she was," Hugo said after a moment. "Only she had a better reason."

"She knew the truth about you. About you and Caroline. Why the hell didn't you give her a divorce? Let her go?"

"You think your mother would still be alive if I had." It wasn't a question. And Logan didn't like the pitying look he saw in his father's eyes. "You don't know the truth, Logan, because you've never wanted to see it. It was easier to blame your old man. So, go ahead. Keep on believing what you want. You hated this island, and you hated me. Wouldn't even take a dime from me when you went off to college."

"Like you had any dimes to spare?" Logan laughed humorlessly. But Hugo was right. Even if the old man had been able to provide financial assistance, Logan would have refused it. Instead, he'd found himself in a deal with a man who some called a saint and some called a devil.

Even Logan wasn't sure which term more aptly suited his boss.

"I don't give a damn if you're still involved with Caroline, if you haven't seen her in five years, or in fifteen. All I want to know is where she was last, or at the very least where she headed when she left the island for good."

"And I'm telling you that I don't know." Hugo's voice was tight as he rose and stepped toward Logan. "Do you think I didn't wonder? The only family she had were her parents, and she gave up her own existence to care for them until they died. She was a young woman. She'd rarely been off Turnabout."

"So you took advantage of her."

"I gave her a job here," he said evenly.

"And you drove my mother away because of Caroline."

"Your mother left *me,* Logan. Well before I hired Caroline. I didn't even know she was pregnant with you when she left. I had to hire a private investigator to find her and it took nearly a year, at that. You were six months old by then."

The story was hardly a news flash. "And you dragged us both back to Turnabout where you kept Caroline right under my mother's nose. Did you think she was an idiot? That she wouldn't figure out what you and your little receptionist were doing back in exam room 1?"

Hugo eyed him, his face expressionless. "Why did you come back to Turnabout?"

There was a pain deep inside his head and his jaw ached. His father was as tall as he. They stood eye to eye. Similar. Completely different.

"Because I try to make up for my mistakes," he said after a moment.

Then he walked away.

Three days without power.

Annie looked over at the boxes stacked neatly near the rear door of the workshop. All orders that needed to be shipped.

Only there currently was no way to ship them.

"This stuff smells disgusting."

She looked over at Riley, stifling a sigh. The girl had already made it quite clear she'd rather have been over at Maisy's Place than helping Annie at Island

Botanica. However, Annie knew the main appeal at the inn wasn't helping Maisy, but hanging with Kenny Hobbes of the stranded Denver Hobbeses, and she'd deliberately kept her niece occupied well into the afternoon in hopes of staving off another episode of finding her niece and the boy locking lips. She'd already caught them at it once. "Fortunately, the people who buy those herbal teas don't think so."

Riley made a face, but she continued slipping the small packages of dried herbs into the dark green envelopes with the silver script. She had already filled a large basket with finished envelopes. "Smells like licorice. Black licorice. I hate licorice."

Annie stretched a piece of packing tape across the last box. "Then I'll try not to force it on you at dinner today," she assured.

Riley fell quiet.

The only sounds were the rustle of the special envelopes, the crinkle of the raffia that Annie was using on the gift basket she was preparing, and the drip of water falling on the tin roof.

Even with the irritation that seemed to roll off Riley's shoulders in waves, Annie found the work as peaceful as she usually did.

The peace continued for all of ten minutes. Until Kenny-of-Denver stuck his head through the rear door. "Hey, whoa, I found you." His face seemed to hold a perpetually cocky sneer, and it was typically evident as he looked around the interior of the workroom. "Got some crazy-ass looking stuff hanging from your ceiling. Anything illegal up there?"

Annie eyed him. "No, but it'd be pretty easy for me to poison someone."

His eyes flickered, then he grinned, certain she was joking. "Cool. So, Riley, you gotta keep doing the work-thing, or is there any chance of parole?"

Riley looked at her hopefully. "Can I?"

And the fact that she *asked* made Annie weaken. "No sunsets," she warned, knowing perfectly well that Riley would know what she meant.

Riley's cheeks colored. She nodded.

"And be at the community center by dinnertime," Annie called as the two teenagers headed out the door. They barely waved at her, ducking and laughing as they dodged the water that dripped from the eaves.

"Sounding like the voice of mothers everywhere." Logan stepped into the doorway.

She jerked. The roll of raffia escaped her grasp and fell on the floor.

"Didn't mean to startle you." He caught the roll as it bounced across the floor toward him. "Here." He walked over to the workbench and set it beside her.

"Thanks." She wasn't going to ask what he'd been doing all day. He'd been gone that morning when she woke, leaving behind a pot of coffee warm on the stove and the bedding folded at one end of the couch. She realized he'd shaved. Maybe he'd done it last night and she hadn't noticed. He was also wearing fresh clothes. Blue jeans that were faded nearly white, and a UCLA T-shirt that strained a little across his shoulders. And his face was positively grim. "You all right?"

His brows drew together for a moment. "Same as ever." Then he looked around at the pile of boxes ready to ship. "You've been busy."

She could take a hint. He didn't want to talk. Not

about himself, at any rate. What else was new? "Those were the last of the mail orders we'd received before the storm hit." She looked over at the oven that she couldn't use to aid the drying process. "Instead of playing catch-up on order processing like we usually do, Sara and I will be playing catch-up on production once things get back to normal."

"Except you'll probably find out there are orders you've received in the past few days that you don't even know about yet."

That was true enough. She quickly finished tying the raffia around the basket and placed it inside the shipping box she'd already made for it. She deftly added packing material to protect the basket and its variety of contents, slipped the paperwork on top, then sealed the box and stuck the label on it. "Ready to go." She carried the box over to the pile.

She looked around the workshop, brushing her hands down her apron as she sorted through her mind for some task to keep herself busy. But her mind seemed far too empty of ideas and her workroom far too full of Logan's presence. "How does your arm feel today?" She picked up the large basket of teas that Riley had finished, only to have Logan pluck it away from her.

"Where?"

She pointed at the empty spot on the storage shelves.

"It feels fine." He easily positioned the basket in place. "How's the scratch on your back?"

She'd had Riley spread aloe on it that morning. "It's fine." The polite exchange made her head throb. "Any news on the phone lines or the electricity?"

"No." He picked up a sprig of rosemary and sniffed it.

"You don't look particularly bothered by that." She drew off her apron and hung it on a wall hook.

"I'm a patient man."

She lifted her eyebrows, unwillingly amused. "If you say so." She retrieved a bottle of lotion from the shelf and stuck it in an Island Botanica gift bag, then picked up her keys and headed to the rear door. There had been no need to unlock the front entrance at all.

"Where are you headed now?"

She lifted the gift bag. "Drop this off to Darla Towers. Then go to the fields."

"They're wet."

"They often are." She closed the door after him and locked it.

"When I lived here, nobody had to lock anything."

She dropped the keys in the side pocket of her jumper. "I thought you didn't like Turnabout." She glanced up and down the alley. For the moment, the drizzle had ceased.

"I don't." He fell into step beside her as she walked.

"Yet you just sounded like you miss it."

"I miss the days when people didn't have to lock their doors."

"Well, I lock the shop because of the cash register and the computer and the inventory. There are just more tourists on Turnabout these days—even when they're not stuck here like they are right now. Town's had a few break-ins, and they are almost always committed by someone from off-island. But the only thing I've locked my door at home against was the storm.

All things considered, I find it pretty comforting.''
They rounded the side of her building and came out
on the road in front of it. Darla lived in one of the
bungalows that lined up straight as soldiers before the
road curved and headed down to Maisy's Place.
''Where do *you* live?'' she asked.

''Nowhere in particular.''

She stopped in the road and looked up at him. The
man was too cagey by far. ''You know, Logan, if you
don't think it's any of my business, just say so.''

''I'm serious.''

She clucked skeptically. ''I don't believe you're
homeless.''

''Didn't say I was.''

She lifted her hands. Dropped them. Shook her
head. ''Fine. Whatever.'' She would not indulge her
curiosity where this man was concerned. She'd already
indulged more than was safe for her peace of mind.
He was only there in the first place at her brother's
request.

She started walking again, steps brisk.

He fell in step beside her, shortening his pace to
match hers. ''Do you always deliver personally?''

''No, but I don't think there's any point in opening
the shop these days. If somebody needs something,
they'll let me know. Like Darla did.''

''The only reason Darla stopped by the table last
night was to flash her implants at me.''

Annie glared at him. ''She's a perfectly nice
woman, Logan. Just because she's having a hard time
right now—''

''Hey, okay. Didn't know you were now the cham-
pion of the lost-and-seeking.''

She huffed. "Would you prefer I was still good ol' Easy-A?"

"You probably started that nickname yourself to piss off your parents."

She wasn't altogether certain that he was wrong.

"It was all an act, anyway. You told me so yourself," he added when she shot him a look. "And I think you're more interesting now."

That comment thoroughly disconcerted her. "I'm not *trying* to be interesting to anyone."

"Some things can't be helped."

"Well, there's interesting as in 'oh, look at that fascinating bug with five legs,' and there's interesting as in 'wonder if she's good in bed.'" Her face went hot. She clamped her lips together, but her runaway tongue had already done the damage.

His lips twitched. He deliberately looked at her legs. Her tan jumper nearly reached her ankles, and she wore short white socks with her canvas shoes. Hardly seductive trappings.

She still felt scorched by the time he looked up at her face again.

"I only see two," he murmured.

Studiously ignoring him, she hurriedly walked on to Darla's place, made her delivery, collected her cash and continued down the road.

"Your fields are the opposite direction, Annie."

"We're almost to Maisy's Place, and I'm pretty sure that's where Riley is. I should check on her. Make sure she's okay."

"That kid she was with reminds me of someone."

Ivan Mondrago, Annie thought before she could stop herself. Trouble with a capital T.

"I'm not sure you should let her hang around with him."

She stopped dead in the road. "I am not Riley's parent, Logan. I don't know the first thing about being a good one. It would be stupid to pretend otherwise."

He looked impatient. "You're the closest thing she's got to a parent right now. That kid is a creep. You should be locking her away from him."

"The only thing that's accomplished by *locking* a kid away from something is turning that very kid into a picklock."

"I guess you'd know."

Her stomach suddenly felt tight. She knew nothing about Logan's life, now. Which was probably just as well, since nothing would be served with her increasing fascination. But he'd once been Will's friend until life had apparently taken them in separate directions. He'd known all about the troublesome antics from which her brother had faithfully plucked her.

"I guess I would," she agreed. She started walking again, only to stop a moment later and look up at him. "Adults aren't the only ones who face hard choices, Logan. Kids, teenagers. They face them, too."

"You're bending over backward to trust Riley because your parents never trusted you."

"My parents trusted me to screw up. And I did. Over and over again, so in that, they were correct. It's not Riley I don't trust. It's—" *Drago,* her mind whispered "—Kenny," she finished carefully.

"The only thing your parents were correct about was what fork to use for the shrimp course."

Despite herself, she laughed. But nothing about the situation—her past or Riley running away—was laughable. "I'm going to Maisy's. Are you…are you coming?"

"I'll pass."

She knew why. He didn't want to run into Dr. Hugo who was often at Maisy's Place. It was sad. She didn't speak with her own parents for a number of reasons. But she'd never heard Dr. Hugo speak badly of his son. "All right. Well, I guess I'll see you at dinner."

"I'll be there."

It was a promise. It was a curse.

Her stomach felt that odd little curl in it as his gaze held hers.

And just then, the drizzling rain started to fall again.

His lips tilted. The breathless moment passed.

She shook her head and lifted her hands to feel the moisture collect on her palms. "Somebody up there must really think Turnabout needs a good, *long* bath."

"Maybe so." Moisture gleamed like diamonds in his thick, dark hair. "But whatever the reason, you do look good in rain drops."

She went stock-still as he leaned down and brushed his lips over hers. Then, with a faint smile, he strode away.

Her fingers touched her lips.

"Annie?"

At the voice, she whirled around to see Sara standing on the raised porch of Maisy's Place. "Sara! How did you get here?"

Sara slowly came down the steps. "Never mind that. Was that my *brother* you were kissing?"

Chapter Twelve

Dinner at the community center was over.

Now that the initial shock of the storm had worn off, the islanders were obviously heading right back into fine form. The generator was humming, the fireplace in the domed pit was burning brightly. There was even a group of people dancing to the enthusiastic—if not professional quality—music being played by some impromptu band.

And there was a smile on Riley's face. "It's like a party," she said. "You're gonna let me stay here tonight, right? There's nothing to do at your house."

"You're gonna stay *here,* right?" Annie eyed Riley right back. "I'm not going to find you and Kenny together the way I did before we had dinner, am I?" She'd found the teens in yet another clinch that had only served to underscore her unease where the boy was concerned.

"He's staying at Maisy's Place with his parents," Riley reminded. "I told you that before."

She had.

Annie pinched the pain hovering beneath the bridge of her nose. She had to stop equating Riley with herself. The girl was nothing like her; she wasn't a magnet for trouble the way Annie had been. "All right. Fine. If they have a place for you to sleep tonight, then you can stay."

Riley immediately turned, leaving Annie to follow. They worked their way through the room, stepping around cots that were shoved together in some haphazard manner that probably made sense to someone, and found the school principal who—according to one of Sam's announcements at dinner—had been appointed to keep order at the center. Assured that Riley was indeed welcome to stay—they could always use another pair of hands when it came to snuggling with the little ones who were having a hard time adjusting to the odd circumstances—Riley barely looked at Annie before heading away into the fray.

She sighed faintly, watching her niece get swallowed amongst the throng. She was no closer to understanding what was driving Riley than she had been when the girl had appeared on her doorstep days earlier. And Annie was getting entirely too accustomed to having her there on Turnabout, despite the circumstances.

Annie finally turned away, only to stop short at the sight of Logan standing behind her.

"Oh. Hi." Her heart danced a nervous jig and it annoyed her no end. Despite his assurance earlier that he'd see her at dinner, he'd been noticeably absent.

And she'd be darned if she'd ask what had kept him. "Sara's on the island, you know." Her friend had thoroughly grilled Annie over the kiss she'd seen. Annie dearly loved her partner—considered her to be the sister she'd never had—but she'd never told her about Logan, about the intense dream that had been her companion for way too many years. Trying to explain what Logan was doing on the island, what he was doing with Annie, had about exhausted her. Following up that event with finding Riley and Kenny in a clinch had just added another dimension of discomfiture.

"Yeah," he said. "I heard about the way she finagled her way across. She'd have been smarter to stay on the mainland."

Obviously, there was *no* surprising him. "Well, Sara knew what the situation was and wanted to come home anyway. Some people actually *like* being in their homes."

"And some people are lucky enough to *have* homes." He closed his hand over her arm, keeping her from slipping away among the dancing bodies when she tried to leave. "What's wrong?"

"Nothing." She pulled at her arm. "Since you know she's on the island, why don't you go *see* her? She's thrilled that you deigned to visit, or do you plan to avoid her the same way you do your father?"

When it rains, it pours, Logan thought. "If that's what's got you upset, don't bother. I've already seen my sister. *And* my father." His voice was even.

"I am *not* upset."

Her eyes were glassy, her cheeks flushed. She was either upset or drunk, and the latter was unlikely. According to the grapevine, Annie was a teetotaler. "Is it Riley?'' He could see the teen from where they stood. She actually had a smile on her face as she twirled in circles holding hands with April. ''She looks like she's having a good time, for once.''

''She is. That's why she's staying here for the night again.''

Logan's gaze slanted back to Annie. She looked stiff. Completely uncomfortable among the boisterous revelry. He knew it wasn't because she felt out of place among the islanders. He'd seen her interact with them too many times over the past few days to believe that.

Which meant it was a reaction to him, or to Riley. Or both.

He slid his hand down her arm, latching his fingers around hers. ''Come on.''

''I'm not going anywhere with you. I'm going home.''

''Fine. I'll scare up a golf cart and drive you.''

''I don't need a ride. I've been walking all over this island for five years now. And I'll still be doing it when you're gone.''

''I'm not gone yet.''

''More's the pity. If you'd taken Riley back right away, then—''

''She could well have run away again.'' He kept his voice low as he hustled her toward the door, knowing she'd be unlikely to resist and draw more attention to herself. ''Which you know better than anyone.'' He didn't let go of her until they were outside. ''Now what's the real reason you've got your knickers in a twist?''

She yanked at the sleeves of her blue jacket, neatening them around her slender wrists. ''You said you'd be there for dinner.'' She looked shocked, as if the words were unwelcome.

"I had something I needed to do.''

"Fine.'' Her shoulder lifted. "Whatever. It's no business of mine. Sara—''

"Sara already gave me her opinion.'' The sister that he remembered as a schoolgirl—bookish and quiet— had grown into a leggy, raven-haired woman who was no more quiet when it came to voicing what she thought than Hugo was.

And what Sara thought was that he'd better not plan on doing anything more than kiss her best friend unless he intended to stick around awhile.

He could have told Sara that he'd sooner turn monk than hurt Annie more than she'd already been hurt, but he hadn't.

The fact was, he wanted Annie. He wanted her bad. And only some whisper-thin sense of decency he was surprised to find still living inside him kept him from taking exactly what he wanted.

"I'll drive you home.''

"I don't need you to.''

"Maybe *I* do.''

Annie went still as his words sank into her. She looked up at him. There were shadows under his eyes. A muscle flexed in his jaw. She didn't *know* this man. And yet, even as she reminded herself of that inescapable fact, she *did*.

As much as she wanted—needed—to maintain her distance from anyone who shook the secure little world she'd created for herself, she couldn't bring herself to refuse him.

She swallowed. Nodded.

Tension seemed to leave his face.

Logan commandeered Leo's golf cart again. But this time, Annie didn't insist on driving.

The moonlight was a thin wash across the uneven road. She kept a firm hold of the metal bar next to the seat cushion, maintaining as much distance between them as she could as they left behind the noise of the community center and headed straight into the quiet night.

Maybe I *do.* Logan's quiet statement circled in Annie's mind.

She'd spent a long time, years, molding her life into something she could manage. Something she could respect. She'd put nearly all her efforts into Island Botanica. She'd made friends, she'd walked the straight and narrow path of responsibility. She'd been so diligent, so focused, as if she could completely eradicate the person she'd once been.

She could manage a business; she could cultivate plants where others had failed; she could finally make her own way in life without fear of harming what she'd loved most.

Yet in the span of three days, she felt as if all of that was unraveling.

She didn't know if it was the storm. Or Riley. Or Logan.

Perhaps, it was all three.

Logan turned off the road and headed down her steep little path. The motor hummed softly as he pulled to a stop right in front of her house.

She could hear her pulse beating in her ears.

There was no practical reason anymore for him to stay at her place. He wouldn't sleep under his father's roof, but he'd have no such reservations where his sister was concerned.

Yet Annie knew, if she looked at him, she would beg him to stay.

So she kept her eyes on her front door as she slid from her seat. She'd barely closed herself in the house when she heard the distinctive whine of the golf cart heading up the road.

He'd seen no reason to stay.

It was so dark inside that she could barely tell whether her burning eyes were opened or closed. Despite the flashlight tucked in her pocket, she carefully crossed through the living room, and went into Riley's bedroom.

She slid off the crinkling jacket, dropping it on the mattress, and knelt to reach beneath the bed. Her fingers easily closed over the hard plastic box stored there. Drawing it out, she carried it to the living room. She started to set it on the breakfast counter, but the silence of the house pressed in on her. Instead, she slid open the sliding glass door, and went out onto the deck.

She dragged the chaise to the edge of the deck because the moonlight was brighter there, and flipped back the lid of the plastic box. She lifted out the three albums inside and dropped the box on the deck. Her hands shook as she arranged the thick books on her lap, the most recent on top.

A young girl's lifetime, captured on film.

She flipped open the cover.

She made it halfway through the first album before the tears completely blinded her.

"Annie?" Logan was there, crouched down beside her. His hand cupped her cheek. "I knocked."

She could only stare at him, her chest aching. Without volition, she pressed her cheek against the warmth of his hard hand, closing her eyes. "I heard you leave."

"I came back." He moved the heavy albums from her lap and tucked them beneath the chair. "Let's get you inside."

"It's too quiet. Too empty." She pressed her fist against her mouth, stifling a hiccupping sob.

He exhaled roughly. "Ah, Annie." He sat on the edge of the chaise, lifting her, as if she were a child, right onto his lap. "Don't." His hands stroked through her hair. "It'll be all right."

She shook back her head, looking into his face. She'd left tears and childhood long behind. "No," she whispered. He didn't know what had happened; he didn't know what she'd done. If he did, he'd hate her as much as she'd hated herself. "No," she said again, and leaning into him, she pressed her mouth against his.

His lips felt cool, like the night. She felt the way his hands tightened in her hair, then deliberately loosened and fell away. "Annie—"

"Kiss me."

He made a low sound.

Her lips skimmed over his. Her heart raced. Her stomach felt tight. Ever since the last time, she'd wanted to taste him again. To feel him again.

She wanted his hands on her. Then, maybe, she could forget.

''Logan, kiss me.'' She twisted in his arms, sliding her hands up his soft jacket, over his shoulders.

He caught them, stilling, as they reached his neck. ''I want more than a kiss, Annie. You're not—''

She moved her lips over his again. Nibbling. Tasting. He wouldn't let go of her hands so she curled her fingers down over his, holding him in return. ''I want more,'' she whispered. Her lips tingled against the soft scrape as she drew them along his jaw. She reached his throat, right beneath his ear. ''Everything.''

He suddenly let go of her hands and grasped her head between his two hands, forcing her back so he could look into her face. His eyes were dark shadows in the night, no less intense because of it. ''Are you sure?''

He'd sheltered her from a storm.

If only he could shelter her from herself.

''Yes.''

He inhaled sharply. She waited, her breath stalled in her throat, for his kiss. For him to devour her, the way his eyes said he wanted to do. Instead, his touch was slow. Achingly gentle, as he brushed his thumb over her lips.

No. She didn't want gentle. She wanted a raging flood that would block out all thought. She twisted her head, restless. ''Logan—''

''Sshh.'' His hand crept behind her head, cradling it while his other thumb continued gliding back and forth against her lip. Then up her cheek, drying the trail of tears.

Pinpricks burned behind her eyes.

He tilted her head and kissed the corner of her lips.

The corner of her eyes. His gentleness was like some exquisite pain squeezing her soul.

She exhaled, truly shaken.

Then he stood, drawing her up with him.

Her legs shook. Her breath stumbled.

"I won't hurt you."

She would have laughed had she possessed the strength. She could only seem to stand there, quivering as his fingertips slowly explored the shape of her face, the curve of her neck. He slipped those tantalizing fingertips beneath the neckline of her T-shirt, grazing the hollow of her throat, then back up again, sliding along her jaw, slipping into her hair.

"You are so beautiful." His voice seemed to come from somewhere deep inside him. "More now than ever."

An image of that long-ago incident at the wedding reception sidled into her mind. He'd called her beautiful then, too. A beautiful *child* too foolish and selfish for her own good.

"Not the past," she was barely aware of speaking the words. "Don't think of the past."

"Sshh. It's okay." His lips touched hers. "It's gone. It's over."

Her eyes felt heavy. Her body ached from an eon of loneliness. "Make love with me, Logan." She slid her hand around his neck, tugging his head closer. The more boneless she felt, the more tensely he held himself. She could feel it in his corded neck, in his tight jaw when she kissed it. "Now."

She pulled at the wide strap of her jumper until it came off her shoulder. Then the other side. The dress was so loose, it fell straight down her hips, piling in folds of khaki around her feet.

He muttered a soft oath and sat down again on the edge of the chaise. His arm was like an iron brace around her back, yet she didn't feel trapped, only treasured as he pressed his mouth against her abdomen, his warm breath stealing through the tight weave of her T-shirt.

Her hands twisted in the shirt he wore, pressing against the unyielding breadth of his shoulders. Her knees would have buckled if not for his hold on her when his mouth ran up the center of her shirt, kissed the valley between her breasts, then closed, open-mouthed over one tight crest, then the other. But it wasn't enough. She wanted—needed—his mouth on her skin. She wanted his *skin* on her skin.

She scrabbled at his shirt, tugging and pulling until she managed to break his hold on her long enough to drag the shirt over his head. She tossed it to the deck, and reached for her own, but his hands beat her to it. With agonizing slowness, he drew it upward, letting her pull her arms free, then tugged it completely away.

Her hair tumbled around her shoulders and for a painfully exposed moment she wished for the days when her hair had been able to blanket her to the waist.

Her skin pebbled in the chill night air, yet beneath the surface, she felt hot. As if her skin had shrunk a size beneath the heat of his hooded gaze.

Then his hands covered her. Shaped her, plumped her to his lips.

And her knees did give way.

He caught her easily and rose, lifting her right off her feet. She had a fleeting thought that she must look silly in only her panties and short white socks and canvas shoes, but there was nothing in his gaze that told her so.

If anything, he looked…he looked…fierce.

Male to her female.

His mouth covered hers as he carried her inside. She toed off her shoes and gave them no further thought as liquid heat stole through her. He carried her unerringly through to her bedroom, despite the pitch dark. Slowly lowered her legs until she stood in front of him. His jeans felt coarse against her, and she was hazily grateful for that pitch dark for it hid the way her mouth opened in a soundless gasp when she felt his hands slide down her hips. Her thighs.

He lifted her ankle and drew off one little sock.

He kissed her knee.

Drew off the other sock.

Kissed her thigh.

And he kissed the heart of her, right through the utterly conventional, thoroughly unimaginative white cotton panties she wore.

Her hands tangled in his hair and her gasp found voice. "Logan, I don't, I can't—"

His lips moved to her belly. Her hips. "Sshh," he soothed. "We'll go as slow as you want, Annie. Whatever you need."

What she'd needed was an end to the pain of the past. What she'd gotten was a writhing ache inside her that only he could quench. "I need you." She slid down to her knees on the sisal rug, hissing as her breasts grazed the hair whirling over his chest. Without conscious thought, she arched into him, swaying against the delicious friction.

He made a sound, a growl, that sent shivers skittering along her spine, and he kissed her again.

Hard.

Her head fell back, pushing against the side of the

mattress that she hadn't even realized was so near. His tongue swept inside, taunting her. Tempting her.

"Come out, come out, come out to play."

The tune dangled in her mind and she found herself smiling against him, her heart leaping in some foolishly hopeful dance that she couldn't even put a name to.

She felt his lips curve, too, and the sensation was alternately unique and seductive. And when he finally lifted his head, their harsh breaths were audible in the utter silence, a song that she knew would remain with her the rest of her days.

She went still, caught in a web of need so deep she wasn't sure she'd ever emerge. Or if she wanted to.

"We can still stop."

His voice was husky.

She frowned. Stop? The darkness made her bold. She ran her hands down his chest until she found the waistband of his jeans. She brushed her knuckles over the rigid length of him that no amount of stone-washed denim could disguise. "Can we?"

He grunted and grabbed her hand, pressing it back against the mattress beside her head. "Yes." But his voice sounded strained. "If you're not ready for this, I can stop."

"Then you're stronger than I am." He wouldn't release her hand, but she had the rest of her body at her disposal, and she arched against him, fitting herself against him. "Because I can't."

He let go of her hand and suddenly lifted her until she sat on the edge of the bed. Some portion of her mind thought he must have eyes like a cat to be able to make out anything at all in the night-blackened room. She heard a rustling, sensed that he'd risen and was pulling off his jeans.

Then his hands slid over her thighs, between them, and she stopped thinking altogether.

She felt his kiss on her knee. Her thigh. Her shoulder. Her breast.

Never expected, a random delight.

She dug her fingers into the bedding beneath her. Her head fell back like an overblown bloom; a moan rose in her throat. Where his lips fell, his hands teased elsewhere. Sliding down her spine, seeming to feel out every vertebrae, grazing soothingly over the still-tender scratch, then pressing against her throat, as if to absorb the feel of the gasping moan she couldn't seem to contain. Skimming over her panties again, slowly urging them away from the moisture where they clung.

And his rough exhalation when his hand covered her.

Her stomach clenched, hard.

Her thighs instinctively closed and he made that soft shushing sound again, stilling until she relaxed once more.

And then she felt his fingers draw through that moisture, sift through that down. She sank back against the bed, pulling at him, certain that their heartbeats were as loud as their uneven breathing.

She wasn't a virgin, there was no point in pretending she was. But this was still new to her.

New and—oh, please—so excruciatingly wondrous.

His hand rocked against her. "Yes?"

Her head twisted. She pressed her heels against the mattress. *"Yes."*

Then his mouth was on her, and everything she

thought she knew ceased to exist. There was only him. His loving.

She cried out, and the bed squeaked ever so softly as she convulsed, only his hands on her to keep her from flying apart.

Shudders still quaked through her when he finally—*finally*—moved up onto the bed beside her. She was barely aware of the hot tears that had streaked out from her eyes, but he seemed to know they were there, and he brushed them away, murmuring nothing as he tucked her head against his chest, and held her while her world tried to right itself.

A futile endeavor.

There was his heart, thundering beneath her cheek. His abdomen rigid beneath her palm as she slowly stroked down his torso.

He caught her hand before she could reach him. "Wait."

She could no more wait now than she could have stopped earlier. But he didn't go anywhere. Just leaned away for a moment. Then she heard a soft tear, and the bed gave that little squeak.

Realization nudged through the desire that shrouded her. "I'll bet you were an Eagle Scout," she whispered.

"Always prepared." He tipped her back and her thighs eagerly welcomed the weight of him.

And then there were no more words. Nothing but her soft cries and his long, low groan, as he pressed into her tight body. Again. And again. And when she started trembling wildly, his hard palms slid against hers, his fingers threading through hers.

He could protect her from herself. But as they hurtled into the abyss, and his head fell to her shoulder,

her body a cradle for his, she had the fleeting thought
that, perhaps, she could protect him, too.

Annie's eyes came open with a start. She propped
herself up on her arm and Logan's hand slid through
her hair.

"You okay?" His voice was husky with sleep.

She listened, not sure what had wakened her. But
the house was silent. No storm raged outside. The
glimmer of dawn had broken through the window,
bathing her bed in hazy silhouette.

"I don't know. Yes."

She looked down at him, and, no matter that she
still felt weak from his lovemaking, her blood suddenly ran streaking through her veins.

His hair looked darker than ever against her white
pillow and his shoulder where her hand rested looked
like bronzed satin. But it wasn't his darkly handsome
looks that made her nerves sing. It was the way his
gaze touched her face, the way his eyes looked into
hers, intensely intimate. Sunlight unfurling her petals.

Helpless in the grip of it, she leaned over him, her
lips a hairbreadth from his. She slowly drew her leg
up his, and reveled in the way he inhaled, his chest
pressing against her breasts. His hands skimmed down
her spine, then curled around her hips as she slid over
him, and with agonizing slowness, began taking him
in.

He groaned. His fingers flexed against her hips, and
she cried out, her senses racing as he thrust upward,
then twisted over, dragging her beneath him. Stealing
all coherent thought but one.

Reality was better than the dream.

Chapter Thirteen

He'd filled the bath for her. And the water was warm enough to actually steam the air in the chilly bathroom.

While she'd slept, he'd heated gallon after gallon of water.

She was still scrambling for composure against the thoroughly unexpected gesture when the door creaked and he joined her.

A practical man who could be impractical.

She leaned up, sliding her arms around his shoulders.

"Hey." He hastily set down the pot of hot water he carried. "If I'd known all it took was warm water—"

She laughed softly and pushed away, tilting her head away from him to dash at a tear. She slipped off her robe and quickly stepped into the water.

It felt heavenly. She slowly sat and leaned back.

Even though she was anxious to get to the community center and check on Riley, she sighed deeply. How much could a little time hurt? "Ohhhh, yes."

He made a strangled sound.

She looked up at him through her lashes. "Come on in, Logan. The water's perfect."

"I heated the water for *you*." He moved the pot of clean water until it was within her reach.

She slid down until the bathwater lapped her chin. Her hand lazily drifted through the water. "We already know there's room for two. I'll wash your back," she added.

"And what will you let me wash?"

"Whatever you can reach," she said, and bit her lip at her own bravado.

He dropped his jeans. "Scoot forward."

Annie swallowed at the sight of him, bravado fading. No moonlight shadows to hide behind, no tangle of bedding. Only…him. Mercy. She let out a little breath and sat forward, the water sloshing.

He stepped into the water. As he slid down, the water level rose dangerously high. Then his arm scooped her back against him, and a small wave lapped over the side of the tub. He reached for the oval cake of soap sitting in the abalone shell she used as a soap dish and held it up between his fingers. "Island Botanica?"

"Of course."

He dipped the cake in the water, then rubbed it between his hands until they were slippery with a velvet-soft froth. "Smells like you." His deep voice vibrated through her back.

She plucked the soap from his hand and—sacrificing

another splash of water over the side—slid around until her back was against the other end of the tub. If he touched her with those soapy hands of his, she'd be lost. "I want to get to Riley this morning."

"Before the Denver delinquent gets to her first?" He caught her ankle and lifted it out of the water, soaping his way from her toes toward her ankles and beyond. "Relax. It's early yet. You wake up at the crack of dawn. It'll be a while yet before anyone's stirring over at the community center."

Relax? His hands were slipping over the sensitive skin behind her knees. "On an *ordinary* day, I work in the fields before we open the shop. Whoa." She jerked her leg back. "Enough of that."

He slanted a knowing look at her, then captured the cake of soap from the water that was turning milky. His legs bumped hers. "Never enough of *that*."

He was wicked, that's what he was. She curled her legs closer to her side of the tub and finished washing them.

He laughed softly.

And she had a long moment's qualm over her ability to keep this in perspective.

They traded the soap back and forth. Cursing under his breath, he used her razor to shave, then—despite her embarrassment—watched avidly as she quickly dashed it over her legs.

Perhaps bathing with a man was ordinary fare for other women, but it wasn't for her. She'd never felt more exposed, or more disgustingly gleeful.

Ordinary. Ordinary. Pretend this was ordinary. "What's an ordinary day like for you?" She quickly tilted her head back into the water, poured shampoo in her hand and started working it through her hair. The water was cooling all too quickly. "When you're not stuck on islands you hate while trying to retrieve your friends' runaway kids, that is."

Her tone was light, her half smile teasing. But the words only served to remind Logan that his days on Turnabout were numbered.

"That's more ordinary than you'd think." The irony tasted bitter. He reached out for the pot of clean water and handed it to her to rinse the shampoo from her hair. While she did so, he stood. Water sluiced down his body and he very nearly scooped her out of the water despite everything when her green gaze widened and lingered on him.

That vaguely shocked, utterly fascinated look of hers was enough to melt an iceberg. He stepped out of the tub into a good inch of water on the floor. "There's another pan of water on the stove." If it hadn't boiled dry by now. He left the room, snatching a towel off the rack as he went.

He wrapped it around his waist. His wet feet slapped against the tile as he headed into the kitchen. The water hadn't boiled down to nothing, but the flame had gone out.

The fuel can was empty. Only one full can remained.

He sighed. Damage to Turnabout wasn't extensive enough to warrant federal assistance, and—to Sam's well-earned disgust—the town council had already assured other emergency channels that they were handling their own recovery efforts perfectly well.

Yet they hadn't managed to get power restored; they hadn't done anything to bring necessities *to* Turnabout.

They had only ensured that the severest injuries had made it *off* Turnabout.

He didn't doubt his ability to get off the island. He'd never doubted it. He wouldn't have come to Turnabout without being entirely certain about leaving it again and the storm hadn't changed that.

So what the *hell* was bugging him about it now?

He exhaled, shoving his hand through his hair.

With no effort at all he could go back into that dinky bathroom, scoop Annie against him and stave off coherent thought for a considerable length of time.

But reality—his reality—would still be waiting.

He slowly unscrewed the fuel can, threw it in the trash with vicious aim and turned away.

Annie stood there wrapped in a towel, her eyes wide. "You're upset."

Aggravated, annoyed and generally frustrated didn't begin to cover it. "No."

Her gaze slipped to the narrow trashcan. She sucked in her lower lip for a moment. "You can talk to me, you know."

Could he? They'd climbed inside each other's skin until they were inseparable. But had they really talked? "I'm not angry," he said.

Her lashes swept down. She gave an acquiescent little nod that made him feel as if he'd kicked her. "I should get to Riley."

"That's it? No argument from you, no debate, no challenging what I say? You just accept it and head on down the road for another day?"

She winced. Kicked again. "What do you want from me, Logan?"

He hadn't wanted anything from her. "I want you

to stop acting as though life is going to punish you if you don't toe some line of perfection that your head has drawn in the sand.''

Her eyes looked like bruised gems, but at least they contained a spark. ''Life's already punished me, Logan. And frankly, I like myself a lot more *now* than I ever used to. Can you say the same?'' She shook her head after a moment. ''Of course, you won't *say* anything. You can come here, play hero where Riley is concerned, get a little action from good ol' Annie, who's more like *poor* little Annie nowadays, and head on out again feeling like you've done us all a service.''

''I didn't—''

''You ought to look in a mirror, Logan. You need help just as much as the rest of us human beings. Do you even let anyone know who you are? Let anyone inside?''

''I let you inside,'' he said flatly.

She looked startled. Then sad. The corners of her lips curved downward. ''I think we both know there's little truth in that statement. Despite what...what we've done together, there are too many things we don't know. Too much we hide.'' She looked down and tucked the folds of the towel more securely around her. ''We're a lot alike, Logan. You and me. I don't think I realized that before.''

''You're nothing like me.'' She planted, nurtured, harvested, and went back and repeated the process.

He destroyed. Once and for all. End of story.

''You let someone in—me—only as far as you deem comfortable. But the rest of you, you hold off. You'll chance yourself only so far. Because you don't want to get hurt.''

"I don't get hurt."

Her eyes went soft. "I think you've been hurting longer than any of us, Logan Drake."

He deliberately eyed her. "The only thing hurting me is caused by wanting what that towel covers."

She swallowed. He watched the motion all down the long line of her throat. Then her fingers flicked the knot holding the towel and the thick, soft terry cloth plunged to the floor, piling around her feet.

She had a beautiful body.

But what grabbed him by the throat was the sight of her pulse throbbing at the base of her neck.

She lifted one foot clear of the towel. Then the other. Until she stood right in front of him, a feast of slender, soft skin and lush female curves. And he had no clear idea of how he'd come to have his backside against the counter, and her tight nipples pressed against his bare chest.

"What's hurting you, Logan, isn't here." Her hand skimmed over the front of his towel, so lightly he wasn't sure he hadn't imagined it. "It's here." Her palm settled on his chest, over his heart. And even though her touch was still light, still little more than a hint of contact, he felt the burn of it as if she'd pressed a hot poker to him.

Then she turned and walked away, gracefully bending down without slowing to pick up the towel. A moment later, he heard the soft, definitive click of her bedroom door latch.

After a long while, he forced himself to move. To pull on another set of borrowed clothes.

He was waiting outside when Annie finally let herself out the front door. If she was surprised to see him still there, she didn't voice it. Nor did she make any comment when they silently walked to Leo's golf cart that sat on the side of the road where he'd left it the night before.

Was she glad he'd turned that cart back?

Or was she sorry?

The sun was warm in the sky as it cleared the horizon; there was only the faintest of breezes and not a cloud in sight. A perfect Turnabout day, hinting at nothing but the coming spring.

The irony felt black and heavy.

They went straight to the community center.

A column of smoke rose from the fireplace in front. Someone had set up several long tables outside the double doors. They were laden with large plastic bins containing fruit—oranges, grapes, apricots. A wide basket held muffins, and steam billowed up from a tray of scrambled eggs.

At least the generator was powered by gas and Diego had a good supply of that down at the dock.

Maisy—looking small next to the two men with her—seemed to be directing operations. She spotted Logan, and waved him over. "Perfect timing. Come help me move these tables. We need more room."

Logan had no interest in seeing Hugo again. But he wasn't going to ignore Maisy just because she stood next to him.

Annie looked from him to Hugo. With a murmured "good morning," she headed inside the building.

Maisy pulled him by the arm and gestured where she wanted everything arranged. "George is cooking up breakfast here. Kitchen's useless at the inn. Perishables have to be used up or thrown out." She gestured at her cook—a lumbering man with a tattoo that seemed to shimmy covering his entire right arm as he whisked a huge bowl of eggs. "Might as well use the generator here for something. Everyone from the inn will be working their way up here soon."

"Along with everyone else on this rock when they smell bacon cooking," Hugo said. He studied his cigar for a moment, then stuck it between his teeth and grabbed the other end of the heavy iron table. The legs scraped against the flagstones as they dragged it where Maisy wanted.

Annie returned. "Logan. Riley's not here." Her face was pale. "She didn't sleep here at all."

Maisy looked up from the box of cooking utensils she was rummaging in. "Saw her this morning, Annie. Just a little while ago. On the beach. She was with that Hobbes boy—"

"Kenny." Her voice was tight. Gravel crunched as she spun away on her heel.

Logan caught up to her in half a stride.

"This is my fault." Her hands raked her hair back. "I should have kept her at the house with me." She broke into a jog, her smooth-soled shoes skidding as she hit the hill that led down toward the beach.

She had barely rounded the old stone sea wall when she broke into a run. *"No! Get away from her!"*

Logan swore and vaulted over the wall, prepared for anything.

Annie had darted between the teens, pushing Kenny away from her niece with a none-too-gentle shove.

Riley was crying. Her shoulders quaking.

Logan had barely taken in the fact that—aside from the tears—she looked unharmed, when Annie turned

on Kenny, grabbing him by the shirt. "What did you
do to her?"

The boy looked shocked. Several inches taller than
Annie, he still stumbled back. "Whoa, hey—"

She followed, looking fit to kill. "Damn you, Drago.
What did you do?"

Logan scooped his arm around her waist, hauling
her back from Kenny. "He's not Drago," he whispered against her ear. He ached down to his gut. "He's
not Drago, baby."

He slanted a look toward Kenny when the boy
started sidling away. "Don't move." His voice was
deadly quiet as he contained Annie's struggle to free
herself. He didn't like the kid, but he didn't want Annie looking up the nose of an assault charge, either.

Then he looked at Riley.

She was staring at her aunt, openmouthed.

"Are you all right?" he asked.

Her expression turned mutinous, and she started to
look away. But she didn't.

She finally nodded.

"Who the hell's Drago?" Kenny's subdued state
had unfortunately been brief.

Annie wasn't listening to any of it. She scrabbled at
Logan's arm. "If you so much as breathed on her, I'll
take you apart."

Logan shifted his grip on her and stifled an oath
when her foot connected with his shin. "Cut it out,
I'm trying to help you, here."

"Then let me go!"

"We were just talking!" Riley's voice rose over
Kenny's grumbled, "Man, she is crazy."

"Talking! You were crying, Riley."

The girl's eyes suddenly looked like wet sapphires. "Yes, talking! At least he wants to listen to me. You just want to send me back home so you can watch *sunsets* with him." She gestured at Logan.

Annie's struggles abruptly ceased.

"No." She finally spoke after a long, taut moment. "Riley, that's not—"

"I saw you together." Riley's voice shook. "I came back 'cause I was finally ready to…to tell you that I knew…but you were with *him*."

"You came back. To the house?"

Logan felt dismay rocket through Annie, along with every other emotion that seemed to pour from her shaking limbs. "When?" he asked.

Riley's gaze cut to him. "You left your clothes on the deck." Her voice was flat. "You were in her room. It doesn't take a genius." Her lips twisted and she glared at her aunt again. "No wonder you said I could stay at the community center. You wanted me out of the way, more than anybody else ever did!"

"I never wanted you out of my way." Annie's voice was hoarse.

Riley took a step back and the sand shifted under her foot. She struggled to keep from falling. "Don't lie to me! I'm sick of everybody lying to me!"

Logan felt Annie leaning out to the girl, prepared to catch her, but she sagged back against Logan at the accusation. "Nobody's lying." Her voice was thick. "Riley, baby—"

"Everybody's been lying to me. My whole life! Nobody wants me around. You want me off the island. My *parents* want to send me off to some school so they can act like I don't exist."

"Riley, you have to know that's not true. They love you. They—"

"They love their jobs," Riley spat. "William Hess. Destined to be the new attorney general. Everybody's always telling me what a great man he is. If he were *great,* he'd know that our home isn't even a home anymore. He always said we were more important than anything, but he lied. Our house is like campaign central."

"It takes people to run an election."

"Yeah, well *he's* never there. Mom's always off getting some client sprung from jail. We don't even…even see each other some days." Her voice rocked. "Even when I warned him that he'd regret it, he didn't care. He just goes around with his big campaign slogan… Truth rises. Well, I know better!"

Realization settled. "You sent the letters," Logan said. "Didn't you, Riley?"

Annie's voice was faint. "What letters?"

Riley looked at him. "And weren't *they* effective," she said sarcastically. The effect was ruined by the tears thickening her voice. "There I was right under his nose and they still didn't notice. I used the stationery Mom keeps in their office at home. Cut the letters out of *his* magazines. Real observant, wouldn't you say?"

"He didn't consider his own daughter a suspect," Logan pointed out.

"Suspect?" Bewilderment joined the other shadows in Annie's eyes.

"I'm not his daughter!" Riley's voice rang out over the quiet beach. Then her eyes focused on Annie. Tears crawled down her young cheek. "I'm hers."

Chapter Fourteen

Annie's legs nearly gave way.

Riley knew.

Dear Lord, she knew.

She moved, vaguely aware that Logan had finally released his hold on her, and reached out to her niece.

The daughter she could no longer claim.

But Riley backed away again, and Annie's fingers curled against her palm. Useless. "Oh, Riley."

"See? You lied." Her face twisted. "They lied. Everybody lied."

How could she deny words that were true? They had lied. By omission at the very least. Annie closed her arms around herself. "How did you find out?"

"Grandma Hess. She wanted to take me out for lunch for my fifteenth birthday, but my mom said no. So she came to my school, instead." Riley's head tilted. "Wasn't that nice of her?"

Lucia Hess had never done an unselfish thing in her entire, miserable life. It would be just like her to use righteousness for truth as a cloak for simple cruelty. She couldn't lash out at Annie any longer for her transgressions, so she'd chosen the next best thing. The daughter she'd forbade Annie to even bear. Annie had never wanted to see her mother again, but just then she'd gladly have sought her out, just so she could find some way to hurt her the way she'd hurt Riley. "What did she tell you?" Her voice was careful.

"Everything." Riley looked over at Kenny, who was watching them all with the wary fascination of a bystander who had happened across a train wreck. "You want to know who Drago is?"

Nausea suddenly rocked through Annie. No. No. No.

"He's my father," she told him. "Grandma Hess thought I ought to know he was finally getting out of prison for dealing drugs."

Annie covered her mouth as Kenny tucked his arm over Riley's shoulders and drew her away. She stumbled after them, but Logan stepped in her path. "Let her go."

"But he's—"

"Not Drago." She turned to him to talk. "I don't like the kid, either, but he's the only one she's not upset with right now."

"How could my mother do that? Hurt Riley? She never did anything to my parents, never embarrassed them, she was nothing but an innocent child! How?" She dropped to her knees in the sand, struggling not to retch. "Why?"

Logan sat beside her, his bent knee behind her back.

He didn't try touching her, and for that Annie was grateful. He just seemed to surround her, keeping her from the ocean breeze. But there was really no protecting her now.

Not anymore.

"Riley can't continue blaming Will and Noelle. No matter what Riley thinks, Logan, they love her." She caught her lip between her teeth, and her eyes burned. "It's the only thing that's kept me going sometimes. Believing that."

"Riley's smart," he said quietly. "She's hurting. But when she found out the truth, she came here to you."

"And I failed her again."

"How? By not reading her mind? Come on, Annie."

"I knew there was something else. Something beyond her not wanting to go to Bendlemaier."

"She probably wanted to judge you for herself. If she'd believed whatever tripe Lucia fed her, she'd never have come here the way she did."

"And instead of disproving my mother's words, Riley only found the truth of them."

"What she found were facts," Logan said. "She doesn't know anything about the truth. The circumstances surrounding the facts."

Annie thrust her shaking hands through her hair and pushed to her feet. A quartet of people rounded the sea wall and headed toward the water's edge, where the sand was hard-packed, and began jogging. Logan rose, also, but Annie couldn't bring herself to look at him.

What was the truth? He'd been with them only a

few days. Already he'd gotten into her pores. But he would leave, and she'd be left with a loneliness she'd only realized because of his presence. She had been surviving the position she held in her daughter's life for years. Maybe not well, but she'd done it, because she'd known Riley was okay. Only now it felt as though the veneer she'd managed to acquire had been wrenched away by a storm bearing Logan's face.

"The *truth* is that Will and Noelle adopted Riley when she was two years old. They couldn't love her any more than if she'd been born to them."

"Why not tell her, though? Where was the harm in letting her know you're her birth mother? She could have understood that you were little more than a kid yourself when you had her." He moved around until he could see her face. "Eighteen?"

His eyes had always seen too much. "And I was twenty when I finally admitted *the truth.*" Her voice was harsh. "That I was incapable of providing Riley with the kind of care she deserved. She got sick, Logan. Really sick. She had a respiratory virus that she could have died from, but I was too broke to afford a doctor for her and too proud to ask for public assistance. If it hadn't been for Will and Noelle—" She pressed her lips together, unable to continue as the awful memories surged in her throat.

"And your parents didn't help."

"Are you kidding me?" She pulled out of his grasp. "They tried to force me into having an abortion when they found out I was pregnant. They didn't want to pollute the Hess bloodline with Drago's. And when I refused, they kicked me out."

She sank down on the edge of the sea wall because

she wasn't sure her legs would hold her any longer. "I had no job. No money. I'm sure they thought I'd cave in and do whatever they said."

"But you didn't."

She looked down at her hands. "I'd always lived down to their expectations, Logan. But for once, there was something that mattered more. I was pregnant. There was going to be a baby. A completely innocent baby." Her hands lifted, then fell. "Yes, I know I was young. But my...behavior...caused that, and I had to be old enough to deal with the consequences. I refused to crawl back to them. The last thing my, my *mother* said to me was that I was so useless that I would be incapable of caring for a baby."

He made a rough sound. "What *did* you do?"

It had been so long since she'd spoken of that time. But it was as clear as yesterday. "Will called in some favors and helped me get into a studio apartment without having to pay all the deposits and such. He and Noelle paid my rent for the first few months. I refused to depend on their charity forever, though. I was going to be a mom. Maybe we'd be poor, but I'd never be the kind of mother Lucia was. I tried to get a decent job. But nothing panned out. I had no high-school diploma because I'd finally managed to get myself kicked out of that infernal school. They didn't want pregnant students on their campus. I had no references. So I...lied about my age and got in as a cocktail waitress at a bar near the university where the manager was more interested in how well you filled out the uniform than how well your job application checked out. I had to quit when my pregnancy started to show, of course, but by then I'd saved enough of my tips to pay the rent on my own. And I found another job where a sexy waistline didn't matter."

"Sara knew all this was going on?"

"Sara was…great." Annie bit her lip. "I went into labor when she was supposed to be taking a final exam. But she'd promised to stay with me, and she didn't budge from my side. Not until after Riley was born."

"Loyal Sara." His voice was tight.

"Riley was such a perfect baby, Logan. She did everything early. Walking. Talking." Her throat ached. "I knew she deserved more than I could give her, but I just…couldn't do that. I couldn't give her up. I was too selfish."

"There's not a selfish bone in your body."

She shook her head in denial. "I was. And then she got sick. And Will and Noelle were there, just as they'd always been. I was so jealous of Noelle when she married Will. Well, you remember."

He made a faint noise of assent.

"I thought she was going to take away what little family I had. But I was wrong. She was decent. And nicer to me than I deserved. And I finally got it…how much Will loved her. She, um, she baby-sat for me sometimes when I had to work. She was trying to pass the bar exam, and you know how hard that is. But she was always willing to help with Riley no matter how busy she was."

"Yeah, they're all saints." Logan's voice was short. He felt a strong desire to choke the life out of George and Lucia Hess, and…when it came to that, Will and Noelle weren't so far behind. "Why didn't they just help you *keep* Riley? Or at the very least, tell her the truth before she could find out the way she did? There's no shame in adoption. She deserved to know.''

"But I'm the one who begged them to take her!" She leaned forward and buried her face in her hands. "I hadn't realized how dangerously ill she was." Her voice was muffled. "Not until it was nearly too late. She wasn't safe with me! Everything my parents had warned about had come true. The only truly decent thing I did as a parent was to give Riley to people who *were* capable of caring for her. Noelle took one look at Riley and drove us both straight to the hospital. *She* knew how to be a mother.''

"What about Drago?"

She hunched, looking nauseous. "He was in jail. I...never told him. I never spoke to him again after that day. After Will's wedding. Not even when we were both arrested the next day."

Logan's world suddenly narrowed down to a pin-point—Annie. Her head was lowered, her silky waves parting over the vulnerable skin at her nape. "You didn't see Ivan Mondrago. Ever?"

"He tried coming to the house a few days later. After he'd gotten released on bond. But my father had hired a guard to prevent that very thing. That, and to keep me in. I'm not sure if they were ever convinced that I hadn't been in league with Drago's drug ring." She lifted her head. "Please, Logan, can we drop it? Surely you can see why we didn't want Riley to know I was her mother. The next question she would have asked was who her natural father was. It was better that she never knew any of it, than to learn that he was a criminal.''

He looked out over the ocean, but all his mind saw

was Annie. Long rippling hair trailing over their bodies. Sleek, shapely legs sliding over his.

And her gasp. The way she'd stiffened when he'd breached her tight body.

He'd been certain she was a virgin.

But if she'd been a virgin until that night, and she hadn't seen Drago after the wedding, then how could she claim that Drago was Riley's father?

The bed that Annie had slept in that night hadn't been anyone's but Logan's.

And that was something that Annie didn't even remember.

"I have to go find her," Annie said. She pushed to her feet. "Talk to her, tell her—"

"What?"

Her eyes were heavy, full of sorrow that ran deep, without hope of ceasing. "I don't know. But I can't let her continue believing that she doesn't matter to her parents, Logan. That's what I believed. And look what happened."

He watched her go.

Then he sat down on the cold hard edge of the stone sea wall and stared blindly at the glimmering water.

The truth?

Even Annie didn't know the entire truth.

But he did.

Riley was not only Annie's daughter.

She was Logan's.

And if Annie thought Drago was a bad prospect for a father, what would she think if she knew the truth about *him?*

"Hey, there." Seemingly out of nowhere, Sara sat

down beside him. "You look like you lost your best friend."

"I don't have friends." Only people he'd hurt. Some more knowingly than others.

She tsked. Tucked her arm through his and leaned her dark head against his shoulder. "I remember we used to sit on this wall before you left the island."

"You were just a kid."

"So? I *still* remember." She lifted her long legs out in front of her, flexed her feet, then lowered them again. "We'd sit here and throw crumbs out for the birds. We had good times."

"Did we?" He barely remembered anything but his mother's misery. And her biscuits had been inedible. More suited for bird feed than breakfast. "Why did you come back here, Sara? You graduated from college with honors. You could have gone anywhere you wanted."

She sighed a little and he saw her blue gaze rove over the seascape. A gaze nearly the same color as the glittering blue water. The same color as Riley's.

As his.

How could he not have seen it? Now that he knew, there were a multitude of resemblances he could see. Her bouncing hair and ivory skin were all Annie's. But the level brows, the sharp chin, the eyes.

They were Drake, all the way.

"Turnabout is an interesting place," Sara finally said, her voice contemplative. She smiled a little. "Some things are so backward. But if we were *really* backward, we'd have been more prepared to live without power. Instead of depending on an ancient plant that isn't even equipped to handle the load we *do* need, we'd have had alternative means. More generators, maybe. Solar power. Or even windmills. We'd have used the gifts this place does have, and the constant breeze is one of them. We'd have a decent emergency plan, instead of just depending on Sam to scramble around doing what he can.''

''*You* need to be on the town council,'' Logan said. Maybe there'd be some hope of the place moving into the current century.

''It's not all bad, Logan. There's a...oh, I don't know. A sort of healing mystique.'' She shrugged. ''Sometimes miracles happen here. It's hard to resist. And for me, it's home.''

Healing? Not in his experience. ''You ought to be married with kids by now.''

At that, her eyes rolled. ''*Now,* you sound like Dad.''

''Great.''

''And we could say the same about you,'' she pointed out. ''But I suppose you're too busy leading your mysterious life to have stopped and made time for a wife and kids. Unless you're hiding them away somewhere for fear they'll fall in love with the island home you hate.''

He closed his eyes for a moment. God.

Sara was silent for a long while. ''Dad misses you, you know.''

Logan doubted it. But his thoughts weren't on Hugo. Or Turnabout. Or even his little sister, for that matter. ''Riley knows Annie is her natural mother,'' he said abruptly.

Sara sucked in her breath. A long moment ticked by. ''Oh,'' she said on an exhale, ''my. I'd be lying if I said it's completely unexpected. Sooner or later, Riley was bound to find out something.''

''She did.'' He told her what Lucia had done.

''That woman should never have had children. Only then there wouldn't be Annie or Will. You know Annie told me once that Lucia told her she'd been a mistake. That she'd never wanted another child after Will.'' Her eyebrows lifted delicately. ''And Annie told you about Riley?''

The rising sun glinted against the sand. It was a sight he'd known as long as he could remember. ''Not intentionally.'' He slanted a look at her. ''You've been a good friend to her.''

Sara's lips curved, and for a moment she looked sad. ''It hasn't been a one-way street, you know. She's been a good friend to me, too.'' She caught his narrow look and the cast of her lips turned upward. ''Don't worry. Nothing like what Annie went through.''

''Good.'' He was pretty sure he wasn't up to hearing what sort of situations remained after that ''nothing like'' of hers.

She looked vaguely amused, then. ''Do I need to ask you what your intentions are toward Annie?''

''You've already posted your warning.'' Which he'd ignored.

''That's not an answer, Logan.''

''It's the only one you're going to get.'' He pulled her head close and kissed the top of it. ''Go find Annie. She needs a friend.''

Her head tilted back, looking up at him as he stood. ''What about you? What do you need?''

The same thing he'd needed for sixteen years.

Redemption.

Instead of finding a piece of it by coming to Turn-about, he'd succeeded only in pushing it further from his grasp.

"Breakfast," he said smoothly, and looked up the hill to where a crowd had been steadily growing by the community center. "I need breakfast."

His sister's lips smiled faintly, but her eyes did not. It might have been years since they'd seen one another, but her expression exposed his lie for what it was. "Well, it's up there waiting, Logan. All you have to do is put out your hand and ask. You'll get your fill." She pushed off the wall and headed down the beach.

Logan shoved his hands in his pockets, and stared out at the water.

Reach out and ask?

Easy enough to say.

Impossible to do.

Chapter Fifteen

The sky above the lattice roof was blue. All hint of the storm gone.

What she was facing now was worse than any storm.

Annie looked away from the blue expanse as she paused at the entrance to Maisy's open-aired dining room. It wasn't hard to spot Riley.

She was the only person there. Everyone else had gone to the community center for a hot breakfast.

She slowly crossed to the small round table where the girl sat. It was the same table where the three of them—Annie, Riley and Logan—had sat the day he had showed up at the shop.

How could a person's life change in a matter of days?

The question was futile, though.

Her saner self already knew the answer. Lives did

change. In the blink of an eye. And in the passage of decades. In her case, the days had been numbered.

Truth rises.

Will had always believed that. Had told it to Annie time and again when he'd helped her out of some foolish stunt she'd pulled to gain her parents' attention.

"Truth rises, Annie," he'd say. "Stop trying to find it the hard way."

And there was nothing harder for Annie now than crossing that room, watching Riley eye her with such a tangle of distrust and pain that it caused a physical ache inside her.

She stopped shy of the table. It didn't matter how hard Annie found this. Riley mattered more.

She always had.

"We should have told you."

Riley's eyes reddened. "Yeah." She looked down at the orange she held. She didn't say anything else. Nor did she shove back from the table and leave.

Annie cautiously pulled out the opposite chair and sat. "I'm sorry I accused Kenny of hurting you."

"Just because he has a pierced lip doesn't mean he's bad."

"I know." She struggled for words. Something, anything to make this better. "I'm sorry."

"Did you love him?"

She moistened her lips. "Drago?"

"Not him. Logan. You're sleeping with him. You told me that you didn't sleep with men you didn't love. Or was that just another big lie of yours?"

She tucked her hands in her lap, her hands twisting together. "Yes."

Riley's jaw cocked to one side. "A big lie."

"Yes, I love him." Her throat closed. The truth of it couldn't be escaped. She'd loved him in her dreams for sixteen long, lonely years. She loved that he'd looked beyond the surface to see what was beneath, even when that meant calling her to task for throwing herself at him. She loved that he made her smile when she least expected, that he braved storms, heated water and made something withered inside her bloom when he touched her.

And she'd love him when he left, which he would surely do. "But Logan's not part of this, Riley." She watched Riley's fingers turn the orange. "When you were a baby, you loved anything, as long as it was orange. Orange-tasting. Orange-colored. It didn't matter."

"I painted a wall in my room orange. Mom hates it."

"Is that why you did it?"

Riley didn't respond.

Annie exhaled. "You know that I used to do everything under the sun if I thought there was a good chance of upsetting my parents."

"Is that why you got pregnant with me? To piss them off?"

She winced, but for once she didn't hear her mother's screeching voice in her head accusing her of that very thing. "No. No, you were totally unexpected."

"A punishment."

Annie's hands immediately lifted above the table. She settled her fingers on the revolving orange. "No, Riley. A gift. Always, *always* a gift." Her voice went hoarse.

A tear slid down Riley's cheek. "Then why'd you give me away?"

The hardest question of all. "Because I loved you that much. And I couldn't take care of you the way you deserved."

"You could have gotten rid of me before I was born. Grandma and Grandpa would never even have known."

Annie could barely stand to hear Riley speak of George and Lucia. But she had no intention of burdening Riley with the knowledge that they had been the ones to demand her pregnancy be terminated. Nor was she going to get into a debate over the right or wrong of abortion.

She stopped the orange again, waiting until Riley finally looked at her. "There was never a day that I regretted being pregnant with you." Riley's very existence had forced her to stop seeking what she'd never find from her parents. Love. Acceptance. "Not one single day. Not before you were born. Not after. I loved you all the while." Her head ached with unshed tears. "And so did Will and Noelle. We should have just told you the truth long ago, Riley, but *please* don't believe that it was ever because any of us didn't love you. Or that we didn't want what's best for you."

"Mom can't have kids, you know. She told me that when she started in on sending me to Bendlemaier. That I was the only child she'd ever have and she wanted me to have the best." Riley's voice broke.

Annie nodded, even though she *hadn't* known. But it made sense. Noelle was cultured, beautiful and excruciatingly intelligent. An attorney. Yet she'd never made any secret of her adoration of Riley. If she'd been able, she'd have probably filled Will's house with children.

"How come you hardly visit us? And you want me to leave Turnabout so badly?"

Why didn't you love me enough?

It was her own voice she heard in her head this time. The endless cry she'd never cried, that she'd finally realized would never be answered. Not by George and Lucia.

"Because it hurt too much to see you," she said, and the honesty stripped her raw. "And to have to leave you again. And when you came here, I said I wanted you to go...because my heart..." she pressed her hand against her chest, her voice nearly soundless "...only wants you to stay. But no matter what I feel, your home is with...your parents. They've raised you. They've loved you."

She tried to draw in a breath, but it rattled with tears. She exhaled. Swallowed. Steadied her voice. "And no matter how mad you are about Will's campaign or your mom's job, or about the garbage your grandmother dumped on you along with the facts, you love your parents, too. Or you wouldn't be so hurt now."

Riley's silence lengthened. Then slowly, she let go of the orange and it rolled off the table. She touched her fingertips to Annie's. "Can I come back and visit?" Her voice was very small.

Annie nodded.

Then she opened her arms when Riley rounded the table and sat on her lap, her young arms a crushing grip around Annie.

And Annie wondered, yet again, how many times a person's heart could break.

* * *

''She's ready to go home.'' Annie didn't move from the couch when Logan let himself into her house later that afternoon. ''Whenever you can arrange it. She won't be running away again.''

He pushed the door closed behind him with his foot and set the small heater and heavy electrical cord he carried on the floor. She'd be able to hook it up to the small generator he'd finally scrounged up in Diego's mess of equipment at the dock. ''Are you okay?''

''No.'' Her voice sounded raw. As if she had a cold. Or she'd been crying. ''But I'll survive,'' she went on. ''It's what I do best.''

''Nice try,'' he murmured. ''You may be a survivor, but there are other things you excel at more.''

''Like wanting impossible things?'' She sighed and finally looked at him. ''Sam brought this message by for you.'' She held out a scrap of paper. It vibrated with a fine shimmer. ''Apparently it came in this afternoon over that radio he got.''

He took the sheet and shoved it in his pocket.

''You're not going to read it?''

He shook his head.

''It said *two days*. That's all. Just *two days*.''

He wasn't interested in the message. ''Where is she?''

She didn't need to ask who he meant. ''Still at Maisy's. She, um, she wanted to help out with the kids again over there. Mostly, I think she wanted some distance to…to digest everything.''

''You talked to her, then.''

''Yes.'' Her expression was too still.

"And about Drago. That you think you were with Ivan Mondrago. That *he* is Riley's natural father."

Her hands curled into fists. "Who else could it be?"

Logan's chest ached. "And you told Riley that?"

"She didn't ask about Drago, and I didn't tell. God knows what exactly Lucia told her, seeing how I'd done such a whiz-bang job of earning their disgust."

"Stop blaming yourself for their failings."

"Habit." She finally pushed off the couch and noticed the heater. "What's that for?"

"It'll keep you warm at night. I scared up a generator for you. It's out front."

Her lashes lowered, hiding her expression. "You could keep me warmer." She laughed humorlessly a moment later and waved her hand in dismissal. "Thanks. I know it would be easier if I just stayed at the community center, but—"

"You want to be in your own home." Because it was one of her own creating.

She nodded. "I, um, I need to thank you. For keeping me from doing something awful to that poor boy. I don't know where my mind went. Well, no," she added after a moment. "I do know. And I didn't want that to happen to Riley." She ran her hands down the sides of her pale-blue jumper, looking so brittle that he was afraid even to reach out for her, lest she shatter.

"You didn't want *what* to happen to her?"

"I never told Drago I'd sleep with him. I never told anyone I'd sleep with them. They just looked at the way I dressed, and the way I behaved, and always thought…assumed…and it infuriated my parents, so I fostered the impression. For their benefit. The guys—I never promised any of them anything."

"I know."

But she was beyond hearing. "I told Drago over and over again that I had no intention of sleeping with him. We'd had a deal. He wanted an in at Bendlemaier and I believed riding on his reputation would get me out of Bendlemaier. When I learned he was dealing drugs, I told him the deal was off. I wasn't going to be part of that scene. But he wouldn't believe me. He'd bought my act too well." She pushed her hands through her hair, shaking her head. "I was such an idiot, such a fool. I deserved whatever happened to me. I all but asked for it."

"It." It was all he could do not to grab her. "What *it?*"

"There was so much champagne left over. My parents were furious with me, accusing me of inviting Drago."

Forget control. Logan closed his hands over her shoulders, turning her around to face him. "You sneaked more champagne, even after what happened between you and me by the boathouse?" He'd already realized that's what she must have done.

"Yes, I—" She frowned. "I took a bottle to my room. I drank it all, I think. I don't remember." She pushed at her forehead. "I...it's all messed up with my dream, you see. But I woke up in my bed in the morning and I was...naked...and my—I felt sore—" She shook her head. "Before I could even get out of bed, the police had arrived. They'd found Drago hiding in the wine cellar. And they came in and arrested me, too."

Her eyes were wet. "He was in the house that night. And...while I was drunk...he, we...God." She pressed her face into her hands, her shoulders shaking. "What's worse? Willingly sleeping with someone I despised, or being so drunk that I can't even remember him forcing me? Lucia, of course, assured me that she saw Drago leaving my room before dawn."

Logan hauled her into his arms. No matter what his life was, he couldn't let her continue believing what she thought. "Maybe Drago was in your room that night. But you weren't. You weren't with Drago. He didn't force you. And you didn't choose him."

"You don't know that. I don't know that! I spent years in therapy, and the therapist doesn't know that."

"I *do* know that." He caught her face between his hands and carefully made her look at him. Her lashes were spiky from tears. "I know, because you were with *me* that night. In the guestroom. I carried you back to your room in the morning."

Her softly arched brows drew together. Her lips parted. "What? No, that's not right. You didn't want me. You told me so at the wedding reception. You'd never have—"

"I did." There was no mitigating the truth. "You came to my room late that night. I woke up and found you in bed beside me." And even after realizing the warm, enticing female wasn't the bridesmaid who'd been coming on to him throughout the wedding festivities, but his best friend's impetuous little sister, Logan hadn't done what he should have done. Instead of bundling her off to her own bed without so much as touching a hair on her head, he'd kissed her mouth, tasted the champagne she'd consumed on her tongue and had dragged her beneath him.

He'd broken the trust of his friendship with Will that

night, and he'd taken advantage of Annie's inebriated innocence. He'd thought he'd never regret anything more. Until now. Until realizing what Annie had believed all these years about that night.

His hands were shaking as he brushed them down her hair. Him. The man whose hands never shook. Who never missed. Who went in and cleaned up situations where there was no other recourse. "I didn't realize you couldn't remember."

"It was real?" She was staring at him as if she'd never seen him before. "All these years, it's the…dream…that's been real."

"What dream?"

"About you. And me. Making love." She stumbled back from him, covering her mouth. Her eyes looked dazed.

"You dream about that night?" God knows it had haunted him ever since. Now he had even more to add to the repertoire of transgressions.

"My therapist said it was my subconscious defense against what had really happened with Drago. And I knew he'd been in my room. Not just because Lucia said so but because he'd left his jacket there. A Harley jacket. He wore it a lot. Was wearing it at the boathouse when you—" she broke off, her throat working.

He'd never been big on therapy. There were times it was required through his work, and he'd always hated it. "It was a memory of us, Annie. Not a dream. Drago hadn't assaulted you before the wedding. You were never in your bedroom with him. He damn sure didn't do it afterward when he was locked up in jail."

She inhaled sharply. "Riley. Dear God." Her skin

went white and she sank onto the couch as if her legs had suddenly given out.

"Yeah." He knew exactly what her mind had finally wrapped itself around. "Riley is *my* daughter."

There was an odd buzzing inside Annie's head. Riley was Logan's daughter. Not Drago's. She blinked, trying to focus on that fact, but it kept spinning away from her. What was wrong with her? She should have seen the resemblance. She should have remembered that night!

"Don't faint." Logan sat beside her, nudging her head forward.

"I don't faint." She grabbed his hand on the back of her neck and pulled it away. "You knew." It was like a tumbler falling into place on a lock. "You'd already figured out that you were her father." She shoved away from him. She wanted to scream but couldn't. "God. The secrets just keep rolling out, don't they? And when were *you* planning to say something? Or were you just going to go on your merry way as if none of it mattered?"

He looked weary. "What would you have had me say, Annie?"

"I don't know. Something! Anything. These past few days, all these years, you've known."

"What I knew all these years was that I'd slept with you when I never should even have touched you. I should have stopped, but I didn't. I don't even have the excuse that I *couldn't* stop. And you passed out afterward. I carried you back to your bed the next morning and left."

"I remember I half expected you to show up at the

police station with Will. He said you'd already left because of some job thing.''

''Yeah. As for the past few days, I started to think maybe you'd been assaulted.''

''Seeing as how I'm such a model for perfect mental health.''

''I recognize the signs. And there's nothing wrong with your mental health.''

''Except I got some kid from Denver confused with Drago!''

''Stress. Riley running away, the storm. Me. It was a matter of time before the pot boiled. It doesn't mean you're crazy or that you're a danger to anyone.''

Annie paced across the room. Stared out the glass door. The surf had risen again. Clouds scuttled across the sky, destroying the blank expanse of blue. ''We have to tell her.''

''She's not going to want to know that I'm her father.''

Her fingers curled against her palms. ''Why not? Because you don't want to be tied down by being one?'' Her lips twisted over the words as she retraced her steps to him. ''Riley *has* a father. A man who—regardless of what Riley currently thinks—is devoted to her. You can't tell me that she has a right to know who I am, and honestly think she doesn't have a right to know about you! We can't just sit here and pick and choose what pieces of the truth to reveal, Logan. For God's sake! Look at what thinking that Drago was her father did to *me*.''

''Drago's a two-bit hood who's incapable of making a life outside of prison. What he *is* is never gonna touch Riley's life.''

"Why? You think Lucia isn't as capable of contacting him about his supposed daughter as she was about telling Riley about me?"

"Lucia never said a word before. What would she gain by doing so now?"

Annie wanted to tear out her hair. "I don't know! I don't know what possessed her to do what she did now!" She'd probably never know. "I gave up trying to understand my parents a long time ago. But I won't let her hurt Riley again, Logan, and the only way to prevent that is if she knows the truth. That *you* were the one I was with that night."

"No." His voice was flat.

She stared at him, wishing she understood him. Wishing she had a single clue about what caused the shadows deep in his eyes. "What is it you're afraid of, Logan? That Riley will blame you or something?"

"Leave it alone, Annie."

She crouched in front of him, her hands on his knees. She didn't think it possible for her heart to ache more than it had, yet it did. "I can't. Not anymore. I left things alone way too long, because I thought I was doing the right thing and I was wrong. *Wrong.*"

He deliberately set aside her hands and pushed to his feet, moving away from her. "There are things you don't know."

"Only because you won't say." She slid up on the seat, hugging her arms around herself. "You're not a consultant."

"No."

Her lips pressed together. "Hmm. I've never met a spy before." The paltry attempt at humor fell short.

"You said you were one that very first day. Guess we should have believed you."

"Not really. Spying's not my specialty."

"What is?" She lifted her hands. "Come on, Logan. Give me a reason, one good enough to make me believe that you're right. That Riley is better off not knowing about you. Because, frankly, unless you're some cutthroat murderer, I can't see—"

"I am."

Her hands lowered. "What?"

Logan had to make her understand. "I wanted to be a lawyer," he said. "And scholarships and grants only went so far."

She frowned, looking confused. "I know. But what—"

"Hear me out."

She subsided.

"I was approached by an organization. They would finance the rest of my schooling, pay off the loans I'd already taken out. In exchange, I'd work for them for a set period of time once I passed the bar exam."

"That doesn't sound so unusual. Don't some law firms make similar arrangements with promising students?"

"What was unusual was what the organization did."

She looked uneasy. "Organization. Like…the mob?"

He laughed shortly. "No. Hollins-Winword isn't the mob. They're…peacekeepers mostly. On an international scale."

Her shoulders had relaxed only a little. Now, she pressed her fingertips to her forehead. "I don't understand."

"You don't have to. It's better that you don't." Cole preferred it that way. Helping to keep justice in a world where justice was increasingly rare was more easily accomplished on a need-to-know basis.

"Do you have a, um, a specialty?"

"Clean-up," he said. There was only one situation that he'd left in a true mess. And she was across the room from him.

He knew people who'd broken under less trauma than she'd endured in the past few days.

But not Annie.

"Somehow, I don't think you mean cleaning with a dustpan and broom."

"No."

"Okay, fine. But that still doesn't mean that Riley can't know about you."

He'd thought he was making headway with her. "Dammit, Annie, no."

She pushed to her feet. "Riley's not going to want a job resumé from you, Logan. You're a decent man—"

"I'm a sharpshooter," he said. "They send me in when a situation can't be rectified by any other means."

Her eyes narrowed. He could see her brain mulling that over. What it implied.

"For…personal gain? Because you love it?" She shook her head. "I don't believe that. Your expression says otherwise."

"Well, you should believe it. I'm paid well," he said flatly. And for a lot of years the life had been just what he wanted. Until one day he'd realized it was likely to be the only life he was suited for. If he'd come to hate the life he led, how could anyone else not feel the same?

"Just because you hate yourself for something doesn't mean that Riley will. If you don't like what you do, then you're the one with the power to change it."

There were very few individuals who successfully left H-W behind. "Pretty words."

She watched him for a long moment. "Maybe. True words, at least. They were your words, Logan. That night at the boathouse. It took me a while, but I finally listened to them. I followed them. So why can't you?"

She moved away from him and picked up the sweater and umbrella sitting on the counter. "I'm going to the shop."

"The shop's not going anywhere, Annie. It's been a hard day for—"

"For me? For you? For Riley?" Her gaze flickered for a moment. "Sometimes work is all we have. That message Sam passed on for you is proof of that, isn't it? But as it happens, I'm going to the shop to see my friend. Your sister." Her jaw tightened. "Riley's *aunt.*"

She went out the door and pulled it shut behind her.

Logan just stood there. The paper in his pocket wasn't even noticeable, but just then, it seemed to weigh a ton.

Chapter Sixteen

Four days without power.

Annie sighed and ran her dust rag over the display shelves. Habit had her glancing toward the big glass window at the front of the shop, but her gaze encountered the muted tone of the plywood instead.

She sighed again and turned away. She'd propped open the front door to let in some light and the bell over it jingled softly in the breeze. It was a softly peaceful, gently cheerful sound in utter contrast to her state of mind as well as the dreary, rainy day.

"Here." Riley came out from the workroom and set a mug on the countertop. Steam billowed up from the mug's contents. "Hot chocolate."

Annie smiled faintly and picked up the mug. A few small marshmallows floated on the rich, chocolaty drink. "You and Sara obviously got a fire to burn out back, despite the rain."

"I'm handy that way." Sara sailed into the room, carrying her own mug. She dashed raindrops off her hair. "Comes from dating Eagle Scouts. Learned how to build fires under all sorts of conditions." She winked at Riley, who rolled her eyes. Good-naturedly, though. The two had an obvious ease with each other.

Annie buried yet another sigh, this time in the depths of hot chocolate. She hadn't seen Logan since the previous day. Hadn't seen him, heard from him or heard *of* him. Considering the size of the island, it could only mean that he was off somewhere avoiding everyone, including her.

And Riley.

She watched the teen and Sara a moment longer. But all too quickly she felt a warning prickle behind her eyes. "I'm going to take this stuff down to Maisy's." She set down the mug and picked up the box of candles she'd packed earlier.

"We'll help you."

Annie waved off her partner's offer. "No point in all of us getting rained on. I'll be back in a jiffy." She wasn't going to bust into tears in front of them. But then she saw Riley's face. "Unless…you really want to come."

The frown cleared and Riley nodded. "I'll get an umbrella." She hurried into the workroom.

Annie swallowed. Then Sara touched her arm. "Hang in there," she said softly. Encouragingly.

Sara didn't know the half of it.

But the threat of tears passed, moved hurriedly along by a surge of anger. At Logan, for making it impossible for Annie to let Sara know the full truth. At the sender of that message for Logan. Two days.

Now one. She didn't have to be a genius to figure out that the message meant he'd soon be leaving.

Knowing in her head that he would certainly leave the island and knowing it for a fact, however, were proving to be two very different things.

Riley returned, and the three set off. Sara was taller, and she held the oversized umbrella. Annie and Riley carried the carton between them.

In minutes, they'd made it down to Maisy's Place where Annie left her protest unvoiced when Riley went in search of Kenny while Annie and Sara took the candles inside to Maisy's office.

The sight of Logan sitting in front of Maisy's desk, his long legs stretched across the minuscule office, was a surprise. But the sight of Hugo Drake leaning over his son with a suture needle in hand was a complete shock.

Annie stood stock-still in the hallway, staring.

Sara took the sight in stride more easily. She slipped around her father's bulk to peer at the wound Hugo was stitching together. "Good grief, Logan. Do you have a death wish or something? Another few inches and that slice would be on your neck instead of your jaw."

A gasp slid past Annie's lips. Logan's head turned and he looked at her.

"Dammit, son, hold still. You're gonna have a butt-ugly scar as it is."

Annie felt her vision narrowing.

"How'd you cut yourself like that?" Sara's voice seemed to come from inside a tunnel.

"Doing something stupid, no doubt," Hugo said.

"Maisy, I told you not to call Hugo," Logan said.

"Rather leave your jawbone hanging out for the birds to peck at than have me touch you?" Hugo harrumphed, and kept working. "Should have gone to my office, but no. Stubborn cuss."

"Like someone else we know and love," Maisy said, her gaze pointedly on Hugo. "Stop grumbling and fix him."

"All I wanted was a bandage."

"I told you not to move. That includes talking," Hugo snapped. "Or do you want to lose even more blood?"

"I still want to know what happened," Sara complained. "You look like you've been in a knife fight, for heaven's sake! Do I need to get the sheriff?"

Annie silently crumpled.

Logan jerked, pushing past his father, who cursed colorfully, and caught Annie a spare moment before her head hit the hardwood floor.

"Good Lord." Maisy swept by him, pushing at him. "Let your father finish."

"But—"

She glared at him, but her touch was gentle as she sat down beside Annie, chafing her hands. "Get."

Sara crouched down, too. Her eyes were sharp as she looked from him to Annie and back again. "You're dripping blood on her." She handed him one of the gauze pads Hugo had brought.

He pressed it to his jaw and carefully thumbed away a drop from Annie's arm.

"She's exhausted."

"And you're not?" Sara raised her eyebrows. "Let Dad finish, Logan."

Annie was already stirring. Her lashes slowly lifted

and she stared up at him. "What…oh, God." Color suffused her cheeks. "I'm sorry."

"Sshh. Lie still." He smoothed her hair back from her forehead.

Her fingers lifted toward him. "What happened?"

"A piece of wire snapped. Caught me wrong."

"And I'm gonna pump you full of antibiotics because of it," Hugo said above them. "Now get up here."

"Let him finish." Annie's urging was soft. "Please?"

He exhaled roughly. Then resumed his seat inside the doorway of Maisy's office. Hugo snapped on a fresh pair of gloves and leaned over him again. "If she asks you to stay on the island in that sweet voice, you going to agree to that, too?" His voice was soft, meant only for Logan.

Logan closed his eyes. "Stitch and shut up." His voice was as low as Hugo's.

"You're a cold bastard."

"Take after my father."

A strong hand closed over Logan's shoulder. He looked up into Maisy's face. Her hair practically vibrated with the anger that lit her eyes. "I ought to lock the two of you alone in here until you can be civil with each other."

"Our cold dead bodies would be discovered eventually," Hugo's voice was dry.

Maisy threw up her hands. She made no attempt at keeping her voice quiet this time. "Idiots. Both of you. You," she pointed at Hugo, "never told your children that their mother was clinically depressed and made *your* life hell when she wouldn't take her medication.

And you," she pointed at Logan, "never saw that your father was suffering more than any of you. Your mother didn't commit suicide because of him, she did it despite him. And you're both a pair of idiots."

"He gave her plenty cause to be depressed." Logan looked at his father.

Maisy stomped her foot. Hard. "Stop. Right now. I won't have it."

Hugo was staring at Maisy as if he'd never seen her before. "Woman, you had no right to tell them about Madeline."

Maisy's eyebrows shot up into her corkscrew bangs. "Oh, really. Really? Sara practically grew up with no mother at all. You think she didn't have a right to know why?"

Her gaze took in both Logan and Sara—who looked shocked as she sat next to Annie on the floor. "Madeline was ill *years* before either one of you children came along. Just because Madeline was too proud to admit it publicly didn't mean that people didn't know, Hugo. But she was a Turn and Lord knows Turns *always* watch out for each other, even if that meant covering for her illness. What purpose does it serve to honor her *secret* after all these years, particularly when it only hurts the people she left behind?"

Hugo rapidly tied off another stitch. The last one. Then he jabbed a hypodermic syringe into Logan's arm, seeming to relish the task as he gave the antibiotic, before he tossed everything back into his case, peeled off the gloves and tossed them in also. He picked the bag off the desk, stuck his cigar between his teeth and towered over Maisy. "You are an annoying old woman."

She glared right back. "You are an annoying old man."

Hugo exhaled noisily. He turned on his heel and, stepping over both Sara and Annie, stomped away down the hall.

Maisy's shoulders drooped. Sara pushed to her feet and quickly hugged her. "Don't worry. Dad will get over his mad."

Maisy patted Sara's shoulder. "I know." Then she stepped back, straightened her dress and shoved her hands into the patch pockets on the front of it. "Sara, put a dressing on your brother's jaw. Annie, go to the kitchen and tell George to give you a few of the muffins he made up at the community center yesterday morning. You need to eat."

Then she turned on her heel and hurried down the hall.

"I don't have the nerve not to obey," Sara muttered. She picked up one of the wrapped packets Hugo had left on the desk and, peeling it open, stuck the dressing across Logan's jaw. Then she brushed her hands down her thighs. Looked between Annie and Logan a moment longer, then hurried in the same direction Maisy had taken.

Annie started to push to her feet.

Logan was out of his chair in a flash, helping.

If he hadn't touched her, there might have been some hope that she wouldn't start shaking. But he did. And she did.

"Does it hurt?" Her fingers skimmed the edge of the self-adhesive bandage.

"Not as much as the javelin he shoved in my arm."

"What were you doing to cut yourself with wire?"

"It doesn't matter."

"In other words, it's none of my business."

He looked like a man at the end of his tether. "Where's Riley?"

"With Kenny, most likely."

"Then let's go find her."

Annie's head swam a little, and it had nothing to do with feeling faint. "Logan?"

"We'll tell her together."

She pressed her palms against the sudden churning in her stomach. And then what? The question cried inside her head.

She didn't voice it. She already knew the answer.

Two days. Now one.

Logan would leave.

Riley would go back home.

Annie would stay on Turnabout, with her herbs and her potions.

Nobody would be together.

But they'd all know the truth.

Just then, the value of that seemed almost out of her understanding. Almost.

"Okay," she said. "We'll go find her."

In the end, Riley took hearing the news better than Logan and Annie took delivering it. She stared at Logan across the little round table in the dining area that seemed to be their unspoken place for gut-wrenching moments when it came to the three of them. "You're the reason I have blue eyes, then."

Annie closed her hands together in her lap as Logan nodded.

The young set of blue eyes turned toward Annie.

"Thought you said he wasn't your boyfriend. Not now. Not before."

"He wasn't. We—"

"We never had time to be boyfriend and girl-friend," Logan cut her off. His gaze met hers. "But we were friends." He barely hesitated over the statement.

"Then how come you didn't know Auntie Annie was pregnant with me?"

Words failed her.

"Because I let her down," Logan said in a voice as stark as the white bandage covering his jaw. "And I'm sorry."

He spoke to Riley, but Annie knew the words were for *her.*

"I don't need another dad, you know." Riley's voice was gruff. Defensive. "I don't need another mom, either."

Annie's eyes burned. Not from what Riley said. She understood perfectly where Riley stood.

Logan nodded after a moment. "I know. You already have parents."

"Makes it easy on you, huh?"

"Riley—"

"Well?" Riley shot Annie a look. "He never had to do anything hard about any of this. He just slept with you and walked. He didn't even come to Turnabout on his own. He came 'cause my dad hired him to come and get me. Dad doesn't know about you, I'll bet. Otherwise he'd have hired somebody else."

"You're probably right." A deep voice came from across the room.

Annie twisted in her chair to look. Riley jumped out of her chair so fast it tipped over behind her.

Logan stood, too. More slowly. He eyed the man across the room. Contained the urge to strangle him. "Hello, Will."

Annie's voice was hushed. "Riley, you can go and find Kenny again. I'm sure he's still waiting for you."

"But—"

"Please."

Riley subsided. She stuffed her fingers in her pockets and walked over to her dad. "I'm still mad at you," she said.

"Figured as much."

"Where's mom?"

"At home. Waiting for us."

Riley absorbed that. Then she sidestepped around Will and headed to the doorway, only to look back. "I'm warning you, Daddy. Be nice."

The adults waited until the sound of Riley's boots against the tile faded to nothing.

Annie had turned around to face the table again, her elbows bent, head propped in her hands. "How much did you hear?"

She posed the question far more calmly than Logan might have. He watched the other man loosen his tie several more inches as he walked closer to the table. "Enough." He warily watched Logan as he bent down and righted Riley's toppled chair and sat.

After a long moment, Logan sat, too.

Finally, Will broke the silence. "Who would think there was this much coincidence in the world?"

"Not me," Logan said flatly. His boss's handiwork

was all over this, and it infuriated him that he hadn't seen it sooner. "Why'd you go to Cole?"

"They recruited you while we were in school?"

"That's not an answer."

Will's lips twisted. "No. It always bugged me that you disappeared the way you did. But I wasn't inclined to do anything about it. Noelle married me, but she'd dated you first."

Annie lifted her head, her face shocked. "What? I never heard about that."

"Yeah, we dated," Logan said evenly. "Then she met your fair-haired brother and never looked back." He'd been fine with it then, he was fine with it now. And he still had the strong feeling that they'd all been manipulated. "How'd you meet Cole?"

"You're not the only person H-W talked to when we were in school."

Logan's eyes narrowed. Then he sat back, laughing softly. "No damn way. You're too public, Will. They'd never use you."

"No. They didn't. But they kept tabs. Cole would call now and then. We traded favors occasionally. The guy's only a few years older than we are, but—" Will broke off, shaking his head. "When Riley ran away, I automatically thought of him."

"You told him that Riley was adopted."

Will nodded. "I thought he was coming down here, himself. I wanted him prepared. I didn't know what mother had done. What she'd told Riley. I only knew I was getting threatening letters, and I wanted my daughter safe."

"But Cole didn't come himself. He dragged me into it."

"Delegation seems to be his style."

A twisted sense of humor was more like it. "Every one of Cole's crew undergoes analysis. Mandatory. More often, even, during the first few years after going in."

"So?"

"So it was in my record from the start." Logan's teeth were clenched. "Logan Drake's weaknesses. Namely the betrayal he committed by sleeping with his best friend's little sister."

Annie's hands spread across the small table, one on each of the men's tense arms. "Stop. This isn't getting anywhere." She sent Logan a pleading look. "You didn't betray anyone. Tell him, Will. He didn't."

"If he tells me that he didn't seduce you because I got Noelle."

Annie's hands drew back. She seemed to shrink into herself. "Well. Everyone's always wanted Noelle most. My brother. My...daughter. And you." Her gaze slid to Logan.

Then she pushed back her chair and strode from the room, not hesitating a single step, even when Logan called her name.

"Are you going to contest it?"

"What?" Logan stared at Will.

"Our custody of Riley. You can, you know. It's only fair to tell you. You have grounds." Will looked grim. "I'll fight you, though."

"Did you even notice Annie just now?"

"She left. It's what she does. Leaves when things get too tough for her."

Logan's fists curled. "You know, Will, Annie's been insisting all along that Riley belongs with you and Noelle. That you're the best parents she could have. I never doubted that before. Until now."

He ran into Riley before he found Annie. She was bounding up the stairs outside Maisy's Place as he was racing down them.

She took one look at him. "You and my dad aren't friends so much anymore."

His life was not pretty and he never wanted any of it to touch this girl. This unexpected child. "Not so much at the moment," he agreed. "It doesn't have to be that way forever."

Her chin lifted, but her blue eyes were swimming. "I shouldn't have come to Turnabout. Nobody would be mad at anybody, then. 'Cept Grandma Hess. I think she's mad at everyone in the universe."

"You're probably right on target where Lucia's concerned. But it's not your fault that everyone is upset right now. We're the adults. Not you. You were only trying to get answers."

"Auntie Annie says it's okay for me to love all of them. Guess that probably includes you."

Logan's chest ached. "You don't have to love me, Riley. There's no requirements here. You don't even know me."

"*She* loves you, though. She told me she did."

The words cut deep.

"Dad's not going to leave Turnabout without me, you know. He thinks Auntie Annie is a flake."

"He's wrong."

"I know. But I don't like leaving her alone."

There was that protective vein again. And she was watching Logan, obviously expecting him to assure her that Annie *wouldn't* be alone. "Annie wouldn't want you worrying." He had to push the words past the unreasonable instinct to grab this girl, grab Annie and run. To find a place where nothing and no one could hurt either of them.

Which was impossible.

His life was ruled by a world that required such organizations as Hollins-Winword, such people as Coleman Black. That world and this one here—Annie's world—weren't made to mesh.

Riley's lips pressed together for a long moment. "I better go see my dad before he splits an artery or something." But her boots didn't move toward the door.

"Don't pierce your lip like Kenny did," Logan said after a moment. "And stay on Will's case about spending too much time on the campaign trail. And don't go to bloody Bendlemaier unless *you* want to."

A tear slipped down Riley's smooth young cheek. His hand shook as he dashed it away. "And don't ever forget that you're as beautiful as both your mothers are."

Riley sucked her lip. She nodded and started to back toward the door.

Then she took Logan's breath when she reversed her steps and hugged him. Tightly. Briefly.

He caught a flash of tears when she quickly turned away and slipped through the door of Maisy's Place.

He let out a long breath and sat down right there on the step. He couldn't have moved just then if his life depended on it.

He propped his elbows on his knees and stared at his hands.

Annie wasn't a flake.

She was stronger than all of them combined.

Eventually, he heard the distinctive whine of a golf cart motor and looked up when the wheels crunched to a stop in the gravel a few feet from him.

"Maisy seemed to think you might want a ride to Annie's."

"So?"

Hugo shrugged. Studied his cigar for a moment. "She's a bossy woman," he said after a moment. "You getting in, or not?"

Logan got in. Hugo set off with a lurch.

"You're a grandfather."

Hugo didn't seem surprised. "Sara told me how things were. About damned time. About the grandchild part, I mean. You're no spring chicken."

Logan shook his head. "You're annoying as hell."

"So I've been told." His gaze slid Logan's way for a moment and there was the faintest of smiles playing about his lips. "Runs in the family."

Logan barely waited for Hugo to stop the cart when they got to Annie's place. He jumped out and headed straight inside.

She was sitting on the couch, the photo albums she'd cried over stacked beside her. She didn't so much as jump or turn a hair when he went inside. "Go away, Logan."

Not yet. He rounded the couch and sat down in front of her. "I didn't care when Noelle fell for your brother," he said bluntly.

She lifted a shoulder. "It was a long time ago. It doesn't matter."

He reached for her hands. They were cold. "It does

matter. You don't really think Riley is *choosing* her over you.''

"No. Yes.'' Her fingers flexed. "No. They're the only parents she's really known. And I'm not fit—''

"Don't.''

"It's true.'' Her throat worked. "I failed my own child in the worst possible way.''

"You were little more than a child, yourself, then. You're not a child now.''

"And it's too late.''

"Is it?''

Her gaze flew to his. Her lips parted for a moment.

"Say the word, Annie. I'll help you fight them.''

"And if we won custody of her? What then? What would you do?''

"I'd—''

"Still leave,'' she challenged huskily. "Tell me I'm wrong.''

But he couldn't.

He lowered his head. "I'll make sure building supplies and food are delivered. Get Diego a bloody boat that isn't forty years old and leaking like a sieve.'' He'd never used his connections for anything but the job, but he would now.

"The town council is taking care of all that.''

Irritation tightened inside him. "The town council would pretend that Turnabout doesn't belong to anything but itself—not California, not the United States—if they could get away with it. It's been that way for at least fifty years and it'll be that way for fifty more. If you wait on them to do something productive, you'd better plan on growing more than lavender and marigolds in those fields of yours or you'll be going hungry.'' There was an old orange grove on the island that still produced fruit, but it was hardly in prime condition.

"I think you're exaggerating.''

He lifted his head, his eyebrow cocked. "Yeah?''

"Well. Maybe not.'' She moistened her lips. "I'm sorry about your mother. About all that Maisy said.''

"Me, too.'' He thought about that carved box sitting on the barrel outside Hugo's clinic. "Nothing's the way it seemed. Not with my family. Not with yours.'' He looked at her. "What if you're pregnant again?''

She paled. "We used protection.''

The first time he had. But not the last. Not when they'd wakened at dawn and she'd slid over him.

He'd been as careless then as he had all those years ago when he'd wakened in a guest room at George and Lucia Hess's palatial estate to find their wayward daughter naked in bed with him, her mouth on his mouth, her innocently awkward fingers circling his erection.

"What would you do, though?''

"Nothing. It's not—''

"If you were. What would you do?''

"I'm not interested in being a single parent and somehow I can't see you coming home in time for dinner and homework.''

"Annie—''

"I'd do a better job than I did the first time!'' Her voice rose. "Are you satisfied now?''

"You did a good job already. You loved Riley enough to do what you knew needed to be done. So stop blaming yourself for it.''

"Well, it's the wrong time of the month, anyway." Her face was drawn. "So stop worrying."

Was he worrying? Or looking for an excuse?

He heard a sudden roar overhead. Saw by Annie's face the moment the sound registered. "Was that a helicopter? He's taking her away right now, isn't he? Without even letting her say goodbye." She scrambled off the couch and out the door, running out in front of her house. She craned her head back, shading her eyes with her hands. "Is it already gone?"

Logan knew the chopper would circle again. "Will didn't come by helicopter, Annie."

"But—" She straightened, and realization settled on her face. "It's for you."

"Yeah." The helicopter bulleted across the sky again. It was circling. Looking for a clearing. He didn't have to guess where the chopper would land. There was only one clearing large enough. The old Castillo estate.

His remaining day had just shrunk down to minutes. Despite Cole's obvious manipulation in putting Logan in the same place as Annie and their daughter, business called too urgently to be ignored. He looked back at her little beach cottage. Less than a week, yet it felt like the only home he'd known in way too long. He went inside long enough to grab his leather jacket and shrugged into it. It, too, had been through a storm and it looked it. Then he grabbed one of the albums and flipped back the cover. Baby pictures. He exhaled roughly and shoved the album under his arm.

Annie was watching him, her expression still as he stepped out onto the small porch. She obviously noted the album, but said nothing.

"Diego will deliver enough gas every day for the generator I found for you until the plant's going again. And Sara's got an electric cooktop she's going to bring over for you. Maisy said she's getting Leo to move one of her ranges over to the community center. The generator there's bigger. She said use it whenever you need to dry your herbs—"

Her lashes drifted down. "I always knew you'd leave. That nothing mattered here enough for you. I just didn't expect it to be so soon."

He left the porch and caught her face in his hands, pressing his mouth to hers for an aching, long moment. "You do matter, Annie Hess."

"Because now you know we share a daughter who will never be ours?"

"You matter just because of you."

"But not enough to make you stay."

The chopper circled again. He cast a look up, watching the Huey scream through the sky. Damn Cole for taking away even the grace of a day. "Enough to know the life I lead is not good enough for you."

Then he set Annie away from him and jogged up the narrow, gravel path toward the main road. Heading back toward an inescapable life he'd chosen long ago and had hated himself for ever since.

Leaving behind a woman he shouldn't have loved, but couldn't regret.

Chapter Seventeen

Seventy-two days without Riley.

Seventy-five without Logan.

Annie turned off the stove beneath her hot chocolate and looked out the window over her sink at the ocean shimmering beyond the sand.

She'd made it through every day. At first counting off minutes. If she made it through five minutes, then she could make it through five hours. Then five days. Maybe in five months...five years...the emptiness inside her would abate.

She filled a tall mug with the cocoa, dropped in a handful of tiny marshmallows and fit the lid on top. It was the beginning of May and entirely too warm for the hot drink. But that didn't stop her from making it every single day.

She grabbed her wide-brimmed hat off the counter

and put it on. She was planting rosemary today. The flat of cuttings she'd taken from the main fields had rooted, and sat on the floor by the door, scenting her house with their distinctively woody fragrance.

The phone rang before she reached the door and she automatically grabbed it as she pulled a fresh pair of gardening gloves out of the drawer.

"Annie!"

Riley's voice greeted her and Annie's heart tugged the way she'd accepted it always would. She smiled and tucked the phone in her shoulder. "How'd the debate go?"

"We won, of course."

"I told you that you would." She lifted the flat and carried it out the front door to the small pickup parked there, and slid it into the truck bed. The truck had arrived within days of Logan's departure. Along with a veritable barrage of other supplies. "Never doubted it." She took the phone in her hand and leaned back against the side of the vehicle. "How's everything else going?"

"Mom quit her job, but she probably told you that already. We're taking piano lessons together. She wants to play duets. How old-fashioned is that?" Riley's voice sounded bored, but Annie heard beyond the surface. Not all of Riley's family issues had been solved. But her running away had been the wake-up call they'd all needed.

"When they bring you out to visit this summer, you can play them on the piano at the community center."

Riley snorted. "Not likely. Listen, I gotta go. Just wanted to tell you about the debate. You know, Bendlemaier's team has been state champions for four years running. My school is gonna stomp their butts next year. Just watch us. Oh. And I got a letter from Logan the other day, too.''

Annie's smile froze. The tug was more like a yank, this time. And it held on, good and tight, until she pressed her hand to her heart. As if that would be any real help. "That's nice. What'd he say?"

"Not much. He's been traveling a lot. The stamp was from Germany. He asked if I still talked to Kenny Hobbes. As *if*. The guy's a total dweeb. I'd write Logan back and tell him that, but there was no return address.''

There never was. Annie knew that Logan had written Riley several times over the past weeks. Never saying much more than that he was thinking about her. And the actions seemed to be enough for Riley, who had adjusted to the news of him—and not Drago— being her father with far less trauma than learning about Annie being her mother.

But then, Lucia hadn't had anything to do with imparting the information about Logan.

Since then, Annie had gone to Olympia twice for long weekends, and Riley was already planning to spend a month with Annie that summer.

It wasn't always easy. Riley wasn't always sweetness and light. She was a Hess, after all. But it was better than Annie had ever thought it could be. And, thanks to Noelle's calming influence, Will had stopped ranting with concern that Logan would challenge them over Riley's custody.

So, maybe Annie owed Lucia her thanks after all.

She'd ripped off a bandage with intent to harm.

Instead, the festering wound had finally started to heal.

"Oh, gotta go. Mom's honking. Piano lesson, you know." Riley's voice was rushed. But it was the natural rush of teenagers everywhere. "Love you."

The phone clicked.

"Love you, too," Annie murmured.

She tilted her head back, looking up at the sky. The sun shone warmly on her face. Finally, she sighed a little. She took the phone back inside, retrieved the gardening gloves and her hot chocolate and went out to the truck.

But her gaze lingered on the tree stump from the Castillo estate that sat in her front yard. So far, the town council hadn't been able to agree what to do with the thing. Until then, Sam had assured Annie the trunk would stay in her yard.

But it wasn't really the stump that she looked at. It was the fresh carving there.

Then she shook herself a little. She spent too much time looking at the darned thing. Her foot hit the gas pedal and the truck revved neatly up her path. She turned south at the road, making the drive to Castillo House in mere minutes. Which was good, considering that Sara was expecting her at the shop in a short while. It was the middle of spring and tourism was ripening. So was business at Island Botanica.

She pulled up as close to the house as she could, and walked around the truck bed, her gaze on the plants. She'd given up trying to cultivate the land near the fence and had moved closer to the crumbling house. So far, a leggy vine of bougainvillea was all that grew.

But it was more than ever had grown before.

She lifted the rosemary out of the truck and carried the wooden crate toward the house. She'd plant on the southwest side, she thought.

"Like the hat."

She stopped. Her hands loosened.

The flat fell straight to the ground. It hit with a thud, and fine soil burst out from beneath it.

"I looked for you at the shop."

"I'm not there," she said inanely. Her eyes roved over him. His hair was a little longer. His bronzed face lean and hard, the scar along his jaw nearly white. And his eyes were bluer than the ocean. "What are you doing here, Logan?"

He stepped forward, away from the weathered house. He wore a white shirt and khaki pants and she thought he'd never looked so good.

He nodded toward the vine that clung gamely to the roughly textured wall. "You were right. You can grow plants anywhere."

"Logan—"

"See you got the truck. It's working out for you?" He walked over to the vehicle and circled it.

"Kick the tires, why don't you?"

He slanted a look her way, dark. Amused.

She crossed her arms. "The truck has been helpful. Thank you. The windows were perfect, the new roof is better than the entire cottage deserved. What are you doing here?"

"I wanted you to have what you needed."

"Well, your conscience can be clear," she said evenly. "I'm the envy of half the island." And hers was one of very few houses—along with Sara's,

Maisy's and Hugo's—that now possessed a generator of its own that could probably power them through the next millennium if need be. He could dislike his father all he wanted. He'd still had a generator delivered and installed, and that was no cheap feat. "So far we haven't had to use the generators," she added. "But you never know when a freakish storm might blow in."

"So, you've got everything you need, then." He walked toward her and her mouth dried a little. But he merely knelt down and picked up the flat of rosemary. "Where do you want it?"

She pressed her lips together and pointed.

He deposited it at the spot.

She blindly reached into the truck bed and grabbed the bucket that carried her tools. She knelt down beside the flat and pushed her shaking hands into the gloves. If he wanted to act as if his presence was not extraordinary, then so be it.

Just because he'd carved their names into that infernal tree didn't mean that she'd been waiting for him for seventy-five endless days.

She grabbed the short-handled shovel from the bucket and pushed it into the earth. She'd barely turned over the second shovel of soil when he crouched beside her. He took a spade from the bucket and neatly fitted a cutting into the row she was digging.

"Don't look so surprised," he murmured. "You don't think Sara was the only one who learned a little about gardening growing up on this rock, do you?"

She tossed down the shovel and sat back. "I don't know what to think, frankly. What are you *doing* here, Logan?"

He sat back, too. Crooked his wrist over his bent knee and pointed the tip of the spade at the bougain-villea. "How'd you get that thing to root?"

"I told you. There's nothing wrong with the soil here."

"Yeah, but you're the only one to come along in forty years or so who believed it enough to prove it." He turned his head, surveying the land behind them. "I used to come out here when I was a kid."

"Yes, I remember. To watch the *sunsets,* you said."

"Before that." His smile flashed, far too briefly. "When I was little. Scared the devil out of my mom. She was always afraid of somebody going off the cliff behind the house."

"Aren't you just full of reminiscences." She didn't care if she sounded peevish. She was. He'd left her. He'd stayed away. Eighteen hundred long, endless hours.

"You and Sara haven't found the current owner yet?"

"No."

He nodded. Reached over and neatly planted several more cuttings, then sat back again. "I quit."

"Well, I didn't ask you to help me plant in the first place. I didn't ask anything of you." Her tongue didn't stop. "Didn't expect anything. You leave behind that tree trunk for me to find and then you just show up here and act as if everything is hunky-dory! For all you know, I could have been pregnant when you left here, regardless of what I said the day you left." She hadn't been. She'd been relieved. And saddened.

Logan's gaze drifted down her body. Slender, curvy. Wearing a pair of dark green shorts that displayed impossibly beautiful legs. The shorts were modest, but they were not the camouflaging dresses she'd worn.

"You weren't pregnant. I called Sara a few times. I know you wouldn't have kept that a secret from her and she'd have told me."

"You send letters to Riley. You call your sister." Her jaw tightened. She leaned forward again to turn the shovel.

"Yes," he admitted. "But I came back to you."

Her green eyes turned glacial. "Don't toy with me, Logan."

"I'll help you find the owner."

She blinked at his sudden change of tack, but she recovered quickly. "Another little trick you can pull from your bag along with trucks and roofs and generators?"

"I know people," he said. There was no point in pretending he didn't have connections across the globe. And maybe he was uncertain enough about what he was doing here that he wanted her to know he came with *some* sort of ability.

"Bully for you." She leaned forward, stabbing the shovel into the dirt. "Don't do me any favors, Logan. I can manage on my own. I should have sent all that stuff back when it started arriving. The truck, everything."

"Why didn't you?"

"It was all from you."

He absorbed that. "You found the tree trunk?"

Her expression tightened. The muscles in her lightly tanned arms flexed as she settled plants in the soil. "Sam made sure of it. You didn't admit that the cut on your jaw happened while the two of you were moving the tree trunk.'' Only the faintest shimmer in her voice gave the slightest clue to her emotions as she glanced at him. "Looks like it healed up all right, though.''

"I meant what I carved."

"Really." She looked unconvinced. " 'Logan loves Annie.' Was it supposed to be my consolation prize or something?''

He deserved that. He changed tack again. "How's Riley?''

"Call her yourself and find out." She sighed a little. "Rising above *all* of her parents' imperfections. Including yours. Now is that all the information *you* need? Because I need to get these in the ground and get to the shop. Sara's expecting me."

"I quit my job."

Her shoulders bowed for a moment. Then she kept digging. "Why? You believed you *were* your job."

"I wanted to make something rather than destroy it." Cole had countered that Logan wasn't destroying anything, but salvaging a bad situation caused by worse circumstances. "But there aren't many who quit Coleman. When he picks you, he picks you to stay."

She paused. "He sounds dangerous."

He supposed Cole was. But the real danger was in a world that had created a need for such men. For clandestine agencies that operated in the murkiness that guarded the boundaries of decency. "He was…" he searched for a description, "…peeved." Despite his own hand in the situation.

She suddenly looked at him. "Did he hurt you?"

Logan laughed softly and caught her hands in his. He drew off her gloves and tossed them aside. "Would you go for his throat if you thought he did?"

Her fingers flexed. Then slowly tangled with his. "Maybe."

Probably. She wanted to protect what she had. Because of the decisions she'd had to make.

"There's no person I respect more than you, Annie."

"Respect." Her lips turned down.

Her fingers started to slide from his. He tightened his grip. "But there's not a lot of reason for you to respect me."

Her mouth rounded. "How can you say that?"

"The facts pretty much speak for themselves, Annie. I've left you alone. Twice."

"Facts." Her gaze went beyond him. She drew off her hat and her hair, longer than it had been during the storm, tumbled past her shoulders in a wealth of white-gold waves. "Facts don't necessarily tell the truth, Logan. You told me that yourself. When I was seventeen, I wanted what I wanted, when I wanted it. And you were what I wanted. So I took, even though you'd tried to stop me."

"But I didn't stop."

"I know you didn't. And that night is still little more than a dream to me, Logan. But I wouldn't change it, because we created something beyond measure."

She moistened her lips. And her gaze wasn't glacial. It was softer than spring dew. Her eyes were the eyes of a girl he'd never been able to forget; of a woman he didn't want to forget.

"Every one of us could have made different choices somewhere along the way, Logan. Maybe better choices, even. Ones less hurtful. But I believe that Riley is exactly where she was intended to be. Not be-

cause it's the easiest thing to believe—the least painful
for me. But because it is *right*. I believe that coming
to Turnabout and opening up Island Botanica with Sara
is exactly where I was intended to be. I may not be an
official Turn, but this is *my* island, too. It's my home,
and I love it.''

''Are you willing to share it?''

She went still. ''That depends. On whether you
meant what you carved on the tree trunk.''

''I do.''

''For how long?''

''As long as you'll have me.''

''Why?''

''Because I heard you can make things grow anywhere. I'm not sure if I've got anything worthwhile
that'll take root, but maybe given a century or two,
you might have some luck.''

She leaned toward him. ''Sometimes a person needs
a challenge in their life.''

He held her off. ''I didn't want the darkness of the
world I lived in crossing paths with the sunlight in
yours. But when I left, it was like your light came with
me. I couldn't shake it. Couldn't shake you. And I
didn't want to. I hated what I was doing, what it was
making me. You'd turned your life around into what
you needed it to be for you. So I came back. There
was nothing about this place that I couldn't live without before. Until I found you here. I swear to God,
Annie, leaving you after just those few days was like
leaving behind an entire lifetime. Sam said something
that day we were out here clearing the trees about not
looking at what the island would give me but what I
could give to it.'' He looked at the Castillo House.

Half crumbling. Not barren, after all. "And I want to give it back this place."

"Restore it or get rid of it?"

"I'm done in the 'getting rid of' business. I love you, Annie. You're the first woman I've said that to. And you'll be the last."

She was silent for a long while. Then a shudder worked through her shoulders. And when she finally looked at him there were tears in her eyes. And such naked love on her face that it rocked him.

He'd come back, and he'd hoped. But until that very moment, he'd not truly let himself believe.

"The last?" She slid her arms around his neck. Threaded her fingers through his hair. "I hope not. The Castillo House is a large house, Logan. If we're really going to do this, I'm going to want to fill a bedroom or two; maybe with a miniature woman who's going to want to hear 'I love you' from her daddy."

She'd unmanned him. His hands circled her back. "You're willing to do that? After everything that's happened, you'd still want—"

"Everything. I still want everything. With you, Logan Drake. Only with you."

Then she pressed her mouth to his.

And it was the easiest choice of all.

* * * * *

Be sure to watch for more stories
set on TURNABOUT, *coming only to*
Special Edition in 2004.

Hard Choices

by
Allison Leigh

BOOK CLUB
DISCUSSION QUESTIONS

1. What is the main theme of *Hard Choices*? The minor themes?

2. Was Annie running away when she went to Turnabout to live? Was she coping, or growing? What has she obtained by making her life there?

3. What do you think Logan hoped to accomplish by returning to Turnabout? Did he succeed? In what way?

4. Could *Hard Choices* have been effectively set somewhere other than an island, such as in a large urban setting? Have you ever lived in a small-town atmosphere? There are obvious differences between small-town and large-city life. What are some of the less obvious ones? Can a person easily move between the two?

5. What events occurred in Logan's and Annie's pasts that shape their current lives? Is it possible for people to significantly change their attitudes toward life? What type of events do you think a person can (or must) experience before such changes can be realized? Do you think those changes last, or does a person revert to their 'previous' selves?

6. What is the significance of the first storm that hits the island? Does the weather matter in this story? What kind of symbolism did you see throughout *Hard Choices*? How does symbolism help display the relationship between Annie and Logan? Does it reflect the less central relationships (e.g., between Riley, Sara, Hugo, Maisy, etc.) as well?

7. Several characters other than Annie and Logan faced a difficult choice at one point or another. Who were the other characters? What choices did they take? Were they wrong or right?

8. Several characters also played important roles in *Hard Choices*, yet they were never actually seen by the reader. Who were they? Why were they important?

9. Do you blame Annie for her decisions in the past when it came to Riley? Would Annie have been more sympathetic if she had fought for custody of Riley in the present? Do you think Logan should have acted differently?

10. How do you think Logan will adjust to life on the island once he decides to return to Annie? Do you think he could have had a life with Annie if he'd chosen to stay with Hollins-Winword? Would it have made sense for Logan to have Annie leave Turnabout with him, rather than have him return to her and the island?

11. Do you think Annie loved Logan when she was only seventeen years old, or was she merely acting out against her brother's marriage and her parents' lack of attention? Did you ever find yourself feeling as if the world was against you when you were that age? How did you handle it?

12. One of Will Hess's sayings is that "Truth rises." Do you believe that is always possible, or even likely?

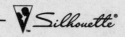

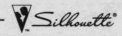

SPECIAL EDITION™

introduces
the first book in an exciting new miniseries by

Stella Bagwell

SHOULD HAVE BEEN HER CHILD

(Silhouette Special Edition #1570)

He hadn't loved her enough to stay. That's what Dr. Victoria Ketchum believed of her former love Jess Hastings. But Jess was back in town—with his baby daughter in tow. Could Victoria resist the yearning in her heart or would temptation lead to a second chance for the reunited couple?

Available October 2003 at your favorite retail outlet.

Your opinion is important to us! Please take a few moments to share your thoughts with us about your experiences with Harlequin and Silhouette books. Your comments will be very useful in ensuring that we deliver books you love to read. *Please take a few minutes to complete the questionnaire, then send it to us at the address below.*

Send your completed questionnaires to:
Harlequin/Silhouette Reader Survey, P.O. Box 9046, Buffalo, NY 14269-9046

1. As you may know, there are many different lines under the Harlequin and Silhouette brands. Each of the lines is listed below. Please check the box that most represents your reading habit for each line.

Line	Currently read this line	Do not read this line	Not sure if I read this line
Harlequin American Romance	❑	❑	❑
Harlequin Duets	❑	❑	❑
Harlequin Romance	❑	❑	❑
Harlequin Historicals	❑	❑	❑
Harlequin Superromance	❑	❑	❑
Harlequin Intrigue	❑	❑	❑
Harlequin Presents	❑	❑	❑
Harlequin Temptation	❑	❑	❑
Harlequin Blaze	❑	❑	❑
Silhouette Special Edition	❑	❑	❑
Silhouette Romance	❑	❑	❑
Silhouette Intimate Moments	❑	❑	❑
Silhouette Desire	❑	❑	❑

2. Which of the following best describes why you bought *this book?* One answer only, please.

the picture on the cover	❑	the title	❑
the author	❑	the line is one I read often	❑
part of a miniseries	❑	saw an ad in another book	❑
saw an ad in a magazine/newsletter	❑	a friend told me about it	❑
I borrowed/was given this book	❑	other: _____	❑

3. Where did you buy *this book?* One answer only, please.

at Barnes & Noble	❑	at a grocery store	❑
at Waldenbooks	❑	at a drugstore	❑
at Borders	❑	on eHarlequin.com Web site	❑
at another bookstore	❑	from another Web site	❑
at Wal-Mart	❑	Harlequin/Silhouette Reader	❑
at Target	❑	Service/through the mail	
at Kmart	❑	used books from anywhere	❑
at another department store	❑	I borrowed/was given this	❑
or mass merchandiser		book	

4. On average, how many Harlequin and Silhouette books do you buy at one time?

I buy _____ books at one time	❑
I rarely buy a book	❑

MRQ403SSE-1A

5. How many times per month do you shop for any *Harlequin and/or Silhouette* books?
One answer only, please.

1 or more times a week	❑	a few times per year	❑
1 to 3 times per month	❑	less often than once a year	❑
1 to 2 times every 3 months	❑	never	❑

6. When you think of your ideal heroine, which *one* statement describes her the best?
One answer only, please.

She's a woman who is strong-willed	❑	She's a desirable woman	❑
She's a woman who is needed by others	❑	She's a powerful woman	❑
She's a woman who is taken care of	❑	She's a passionate woman	❑
She's an adventurous woman	❑	She's a sensitive woman	❑

7. The following statements describe types or genres of books that you may be
interested in reading. Pick *up to 2 types* of books that you are most interested in.

I like to read about truly romantic relationships	❑
I like to read stories that are sexy romances	❑
I like to read romantic comedies	❑
I like to read a romantic mystery/suspense	❑
I like to read about romantic adventures	❑
I like to read romance stories that involve family	❑
I like to read about a romance in times or places that I have never seen	❑
Other: _____	❑

*The following questions help us to group your answers with those readers who are
similar to you. Your answers will remain confidential.*

8. Please record your year of birth below.

19 _____

9. What is your marital status?

single ❑   married ❑   common-law ❑   widowed ❑
divorced/separated ❑

10. Do you have children 18 years of age or younger currently living at home?

yes ❑   no ❑

11. Which of the following best describes your employment status?

employed full-time or part-time ❑   homemaker ❑   student ❑
retired ❑   unemployed ❑

12. Do you have access to the Internet from either home or work?

yes ❑   no ❑

13. Have you ever visited eHarlequin.com?

yes ❑   no ❑

14. What state do you live in?

_____

15. Are you a member of Harlequin/Silhouette Reader Service?

yes ❑   Account # _____   no ❑   MRQ403SSE-1B